Evernight Publishing

www.evernightpublishing.com

SAM CRESCENT

Copyright© 2014

Sam Crescent

ISBN: 978-1-77130-632-4

Editor: Karyn White

Cover Artist: Sour Cherry Designs

ALL RIGHTS RESERVED

LASH

DEDICATION

Thank you to Evernight for giving Lash a home and also to my readers. Your support is amazing and I appreciate everything you do.

LASH

LASH

The Skulls, 1

Sam Crescent

Copyright © 2013

Chapter One

Angel Marston continued to clean away the mess on the floors of the biker bar where she worked. The place was a real shithole, and she wished there was something else for her to do other than clean away beer bottles and the occasional used condom wrapper. Whatever happened in the club stayed in the club, and no one spoke. It was the biker club that ruled the town. No one was under any illusions that the sheriff's office had any such control. They didn't. If you wanted something done, you made sure to see the president of the club or you'd never see any kind of justice.

The Skulls controlled the town, and if anyone had a beef with another person they came here to get it sorted out. The crime rate was down, and no one gave a shit about the occasional beating they witnessed in the middle of Fort Wills. They were a small town situated off the beaten track. The town made money through the club and a few investments in the land markings around the area.

The Skulls were not commercial trading, and they were not about the niceness that the Law Castle Bad Boys were known for. The Skulls were a real bad-ass biker club. They worked hard, played harder, and sometimes someone got beat or killed. Letting out a sigh, Angel leaned over the bar to grab the cleaning cloth and bacterial spray. The skirt she wore was down to her knees even though the club demanded miniskirts that only covered the ass. She, however, wasn't here working willingly. No, The Skulls had taken her as a down payment for one of her father's debts. While she worked for them, lived under their roof, and was seen around Fort Wills, then her father had to keep paying up the money he owed. Angel didn't really know why her father had gone to them for money. Her mother, before she died, had set them up with plenty on the royalty payments from the books she had published.

Instead, her father wasted all the funds, borrowed money he couldn't pay back, and then she got taken as collateral in the process. She hadn't spoken to any of her friends, not that she had any, and when she left the bar she was escorted by a Prospect.

God, she hated her life more than ever. Turning around, she ignored the heavy metal music playing out and started wiping the tables down.

Several other girls were lying around or fucking some of the club members. Angel ignored them. There was nothing else for her to do other than clean, wait, and then get sent to her room when all was done.

Moans filled the air as she passed tables. Angel kept her gaze down not wanting to see what they were doing. She was nineteen and hadn't been with a guy intimately. Sex wasn't something easy for her.

"Oh, baby, you've got a big cock. I love your cock."

Rolling her eyes, she picked up a beer bottle she'd missed and made her way to the bar. Mikey, one of the older members of the club, smiled at her as she passed. She nodded her head, finding it easier not to interact with them. They didn't like her, and she'd gotten that from the glares and the sneers as they watched her. She didn't understand why they hated her. Before she'd been taken from her home, without packing anything, Angel had never spoken to one of The Skulls, apart from the few she'd been in school with, but that was before they became official members, or patched in. She would never understand the lingo and hoped never to.

All Angel hoped for was her father to pay his debt so she could leave. Her hopes for her father paying his debts were diminishing every passing day. She'd been allowed a few phone calls with him, and each time he always told her to make the most of her situation and that he was only human. He'd also hinted for her to try to use her body, big though it was, to cut him some slack. What kind of father asked that of his child? There was a time when she'd loved being around her father. Now, she didn't even know if she wanted him to live with the way he spoke to her. He'd told her there were worst fates than being with a Skull. She should learn to do something to help him out. The insults kept getting worse, and she dreaded his phone calls. She never asked for him to get in touch anymore either. Glancing around the club again she let out a sigh. The late nights, the sex, and everything around them were really starting to get to her. She hated it.

"You know, it would go a lot easier for you if you were nice to the guys," Mikey said, handing her a glass of lemonade.

She took the drink he offered. "Thank you."

Standing behind the bar, she sipped from the straw and didn't say a word. Angel found it easier to keep her thoughts to herself rather than talk with anyone.

"Being closed off is not going to help your cause, sweetheart."

Turning to look at the older man she wondered what to say to him. "I have no idea what to say. I'm here, and I don't know what to say." Staring down at her feet she felt heat fill her cheeks. The only people who were nice to her were the men's women, "old ladies", she'd heard them called. None of the women looked all that old, and neither did the men. Mikey was in his forties, and that wasn't old at all.

"You're too fucking young to be here," Mikey said, shaking his head and walking away.

There was nothing for her to say. She sat down, sipped her drink, and waited for more work to be done. It wasn't over until she was ordered to go to her room. Any of them could order her to go there. None of the men hurt her physically. Sometimes they called her names, but she was used to that. Name calling was nothing new to her. Biting her lip, she tapped her hand on the counter wishing she was anywhere but at the bar.

"Why do you keep her around if she's no one?" A dyed blonde sat at the bar laughing up at Nash. The blonde was Kate, and Angel had gone to school with her. Nash, one of the members, sat beside her.

"She's business, baby. Keep your little nose out of it."

"How can *Angel* be business? She's fat. A fatty frumpy bitch."

Angel cringed. She hated her name. Her mother had felt she was an angel seeing as she wasn't supposed to have ever gotten pregnant according to the doctors. So her mother had decided to name her "Angel" to celebrate.

Nash grabbed Kate's neck, roughly.

"It's business. You want to last around here then you keep that mouth open for other things besides talking, like my dick. Got it?"

Kate smiled adoringly at him even as Angel winced from the rough way he was treating her. The women really loved it here, and she didn't get it. Her parents were never violent to each other. She'd seen the way the bikers had treated women, and she never wanted to be on the receiving end of their attention. The "old ladies" never got such treatment. They were the few women who were not treated like convenient holes, and she'd never seen any of the married men with another woman.

Angel tried her hardest to stay unnoticed. She was one of the few big women who worked inside the club. Cringing at her own thoughts directed at her body, Angel tried to blank out their conversation.

"I'm good with my mouth," Kate said, licking a line up the side of his face.

"Get her away from my bar." Micky shoved Kate's arm off the counter so the woman went sprawling to the floor.

"Mikey, what the fuck?" Nash cursed the barman then left the bar. Mikey was old school and demanded respect.

"You're just going to let him do that to me?" Angel heard the other woman whining as Nash did everything he could to push her away.

"He's one of the original members. Shut your trap if you don't want to cause a problem."

When they were far enough away Angel glanced up to see Mikey stood beside her. She twirled the straw in her glass and tried her best not to look away. Even with

Mikey's advanced years he had the ability to be frightening, or at least to her he was.

He cupped her cheek, tilting her head back to look at him. There was nothing sexual in his touch. Mickey seemed to look at her with parental affection, which she didn't understand.

"You may be here because of your deadbeat dad, but don't let anyone ever make you feel less than you are. Angel, you're a beautiful, young woman, and if I was twenty years younger I'd make a play for you. As it is, I'm not, but don't let a dirty fucker ruin you."

He tapped her cheek and walked away. Angel frowned, wondering what had made him speak such words to her.

Sipping on her drink Angel closed her eyes wishing she was anywhere but inside the club.
****

If Angel kept sucking on her straw Lash wasn't going to be able to control the urge to claim her. He'd been watching her for a long time, and he'd done everything in his power to protect her from her own father. Still, club rules were club rules, and if he didn't make a play for her soon it was only a matter of time before someone else did, or Tiny collected the debt sending Angel back out into the town alone.

He didn't like the thought of her alone out in the world without him. There were too many men to keep away from her.

His brother, Nash, stumbled over toward him. Nash's jeans were partially open, and he knew Kate had given Nash a blow job in the last few minutes.

"What's up with you?" Lash asked, turning his attention back to Angel. Mikey was keeping an eye on her and always did when she was working the bar.

"I'm good, man. I just got my dick sucked, and the bitch swallowed. No mess and I can walk away. I love women who don't want forever. That shit is always a drag." Nash folded his arms looking proud.

Where his brother wasn't looking for commitment, Lash was staring at commitment across the bar. He turned his attention back to his woman. Angel was completely out of place in The Skulls bar. She would be out of place as his old lady, too, but she was the woman he wanted and intended to keep. Angel's long chestnut brown hair was pulled into a ponytail, but the locks looked silken as they glistened in the light. He'd not had the pleasure of touching her hair or her body, but he would. Lash wasn't going to let that opportunity pass. Her body was also out of place in the bar. She was the only real woman with large tits, thick hips and thighs, and a small waist. Most of the women were slim with fake breasts or nothing in that department to rave about. Looking at Angel had Lash's cock thicken with renewed need. He wasn't a small man at all. Being over six feet tall with plenty of muscle he needed a woman to be able to take him.

The women he'd fucked at the club would often complain about his strength, and he'd seen the bruises he'd left behind because of the pounding he'd given them. He needed a woman who could take his strength, and Angel looked like the woman to be able to do that. Not only was her body calling to him, but her innocence surrounded her. She was the only woman in the club who hadn't fucked a member, and he liked that.

Lash wasn't any kind of man to talk about innocence. He'd been a member of the Skulls since he was a Prospect, and after two years of showing his loyalty he'd become a full member. He was the muscle and worked out hard to keep in shape to protect their group. The Skulls protected their town and made sure nothing bad went down. If it did, the problem landed on him.

In all that time he'd fucked plenty of women, and he'd been with a couple who were now old ladies to some of the guys. No, he wasn't going to have a woman by his side that'd been with the rest of the club. It was not going to happen. He was a selfish, possessive type, and he accepted that.

"Kate's good for her blows." Lash didn't tear his gaze away from Angel. She was sucking on her straw with her eyes closed. He wondered what she was thinking about. The club was dying down for the night, and it was only a matter of time before Mikey sent her to her room. The room that was next to his, and he listened to her at night as she moved around. He thought about crossing the distance and staking his claim. Each time he moved toward that door, he found himself hesitating.

The last thing he wanted was for her to look at him with disgust or with fear. Angel had been protected from The Skulls for a long time. Her father, David, was the only reason she was here now. The bastard had spent all of her mother's money gambling and through bad investments. Taking the loan was the best and worst decision David had ever made. Bad for her father but good for Lash as it gave him what he needed, Angel close.

He'd spoken to Tiny and the rest of the club members about what he wanted. They were fine, and even Tiny was okay with it even though they didn't think Angel could hack it being in the Club. This was who he was, and nothing would ever change that.

"All you do is stand and watch her. You've not taken a woman in over a year. You must be begging to let off some steam. Go and take her already. Tiny is going to start getting angry. She's been at the club for a long time, and you've not made a play for her. He's not going to curb the guys' behaviour for much longer, Lash."

Tiny was the club leader, and at Lash's request he'd made sure no parties were out of control.

Looking back over his request to the club Lash knew he'd asked for so much. The Club was his family. Tiny had taken him and his brother under his wing when their family died in a turf war with another Club. Tiny raised them from the time they were boys all the way until now. He'd been the man to give them the names, Lash and Nash, stupid names but way better than the ones on their birth certificate. They both earned their right to be in The Skulls, but Tiny's patience would only go so far.

"She's different."

"Yeah, she's a virgin and a civilian. Of course she's different." Nash let out a frustrated sigh. "You'll never find her giving club members a blow job or a free ride. She's a good girl. You always said you wanted a good girl. She's right there, under your nose, and you're not doing anything about it."

Lash couldn't argue with his brother.

"I'm going to find a piece of ass for the night. Good luck with whatever you've got planned."

Nash walked away without another word.

Looking over at the woman he'd claimed for his own, Lash watched as she stood up and moved to wash the glass up and toss the straw in the trash.

She was way out of his league but the only woman he wanted. He was Lash, the muscle and a member of The Skulls.

Watching her was out of the question. The only thing he wanted in life was standing right in front of him.

He wasn't going to let any more time pass. Angel was his for the taking.

Chapter Two

Angel rinsed out her glass and felt a presence behind her seconds before a hand reached around to turn off the tap. She didn't recognise the arm, but it was covered in tattoos. There was a snake wrapped around a sword down the arm. Angel noticed several of the members held the same kind of tattoo. She paused, waiting for the man to say whatever he wanted to say or to leave.

He did neither. The man stood behind her, close enough that his breath brushed along the nape of her neck, without speaking.

The hand left the tap and travelled up her arm. The pads of his fingers felt like a caress over her skin. She didn't know what to do and stood still. None of the men touched her, but this man was touching her and the simple caress of his fingers was igniting a path of fire along her arm.

Her nipples tightened, and heat swamped her pussy. She'd never felt anything like it. The pleasure was immense, and in that moment she didn't want it to stop.

From the simple touch Angel forgot about where she was. She forgot about the fact she was a virgin and her life was owned by a rough, bike riding club. Never in all of her nineteen years had she felt anything so pleasurable, and all the man was doing was caressing her arm.

"You shouldn't be washing the dishes," he said, whispering against her ear.

Closing her eyes, Angel willed for herself to gain control of the situation. Whoever the man was behind her, he was tall, and his body made her feel small.

"It's my job. I have to clean after everyone."

"No, you don't. You clean the tables to keep yourself busy. Tiny gave you the job to keep you occupied." The man's hand left her arm and settled on her waist. He rubbed against her ass, and she wasn't stupid. She did well in school, and knew he was rubbing his very erect cock against her ass.

Angel couldn't help her response. She tensed. No man had ever come near her in such a blatant, possessive way. Nor had she ever felt so desired in her life. His hand left her waist and moved to her stomach, which was rounded.

"Sh, don't be scared, baby. I'm never going to hurt you."

"Lash?" Mikey interrupted the moment. Pulling out of Lash's arms she turned to see the large man was in fact behind her.

She knew who he was and had seen him around Fort Wills plenty of times. He was the muscle of The Skulls, and he was downright sexy even with the scar down the left side of his face.

"What, Mikey?" Lash asked, without taking his eyes away from her.

Her heart pounded rapidly inside her chest.

"Are you sure you know what you're doing?"

"Perfectly. It's time, and I've waited long enough. You know Tiny's patience will only last so long," Lash said.

The two men were having a conversation between her. Angel didn't have a clue what they were talking about and stayed silent. She'd learned never to interrupt and never to interfere. It was easy to always be silent and stare at the floor.

"Be careful. That kind of sweetness is hard to come by," Mikey said.

"I will. I'll be here more often. You won't have to worry about watching anymore."

The men were even speaking in code, or at least it sounded like they were.

"I'll always watch."

She glanced up in time to see Mikey smile down at her. "Take care, sweetness."

The older man walked away. During their conversation Lash hadn't taken his hands off her. His palm rested against her thick stomach, and Angel couldn't help but make a comparison between her body and the other women she'd seen around the bar.

"You've got a protector. I like that," Lash said, against her ear.

Angel looked around the bar to see if anyone noticed them. No one looked in their direction. She didn't fight Lash even when he started to move her away from the bar. He took her around the back and up a set of steps.

The touch around her stomach was light, but she sensed the strength within his grip.

"Where are we going?" she asked.

"Somewhere quiet where we won't be disturbed."

Her heart raced. The tone of his voice made goose-bumps erupt all over her arms.

"Why?"

"Because I've waited long enough. I need you to myself."

She didn't understand his tone. It was strange and sounded possessive and as if he'd been waiting for a chance to get her alone.

Why?

Angel knew she wasn't anything special, and she certainly wasn't a beautiful woman with a slim figure.

When they made it to her room she tensed. Lash pushed open the door and still with a hand around her waist, he shut and locked the door. They were alone in her room. She lived out of her suitcase, and the case was open in the corner.

"You haven't unpacked?" he asked.

"No."

What else was she supposed to say?

He moved to the bed, forced her to sit down and then went to her suitcase. She watched as he pulled her clothes out, moving to the wardrobe.

"Why are you putting my clothes away?" she asked.

"This is your home. You need your clothes hanging up."

"I'm not staying here. When my Dad makes the money—" Angel didn't get chance to finish her sentence. Her faith in her father was not all that great.

"Your Dad will never make the money in time. He's fallen so far behind he'd be lucky to get out of this year with his life, let alone debt free. His ass is owned by the club. Live with it, Angel."

She shook her head. What he was saying was wrong even though she knew it in her heart to be true. Faced with the truth by Lash, she fought to hold on to what little belief she held in her father. There's no way her father couldn't get the money back. He promised her when she left he would get the money and get her back, so she had to try to believe it of him. Not once, when her mother was alive, had she doubted her father, and now this large, sexy, domineering man was telling her that her father would never get the money and she'd never get out of here, and it was all too much.

He finished putting her few clothes up and then grabbed her underwear to place them inside a drawer.

Finished, he turned back to her. His arms were thick and covered in tattoos. He wore a black vest with a pair of black jeans.

His hands rested on hips as he stared at her.

"Will you kill my Dad?" she asked, staring at her hands where they rested on her legs. This was the first time she'd had a long conversation with any member of The Skulls.

"Not if he works for us and if you remain in our care."

"Care? You call this care?" She bit down on her lip trying to stop herself from speaking. Talking out of turn was not allowed.

He took a seat next to her and caressed her cheek. The moment he touched her heat filled her body. His touch made her want so much more. No man had affected her in such a way, and she was terrified of what that meant.

****

Lash turned her to look at him. Her green eyes cut a path straight to his heart. He didn't know what it was about this woman that stopped him in his tracks, but from the first moment he laid eyes on her, Lash hadn't been able to stop thinking about her.

The feelings were intense and all-consuming.

Seeing her suitcase filled in the corner angered him. Now her clothes were hung up, and he intended to move them into his room soon.

Angel wasn't leaving the club or his side, and soon he'd have her in him home, by his side as his wife.

"What would you call it?" he asked.

She shook her head, trying to pull away from his touch. Lash stayed by her side, refusing to leave and stopping her from pulling out of his touch.

"Talk to me."

21

"How can I talk to you? You're one of the members who are keeping me here."

She closed her eyes, took several deep breaths. All the time Lash watched her. He couldn't get enough of her, and the possessive feeling inside him only intensified with every passing minute.

"I'm not like those girls. I don't sleep with guys, and I don't use my body for anyone." Angel tucked her hair behind her ear.

Lash turned her around and slowly unbound her hair until it fell around her shoulders in delightful waves. For the first time, Lash ran his fingers through her hair, relishing the feel of the silken waves sliding through his fingers.

He liked the fact she didn't argue. Angel did as he wanted without comment. Did she know how addictive her response was to him? Lash wanted to push her to see how far she'd allow him to go.

She was only nineteen whereas he was in his late twenties, twenty-nine to be exact.

"I know, Angel. I know you wouldn't get on your knees if one of the guys asked you to. You've never known what it's like to feel a cock inside you. This world is entirely new to you. I get it. You may not think I do, but I do."

The blush stained her cheeks, and he saw it when he turned her around. He wasn't going to hide who he was. Lash had already done everything he could to make her life at the club bearable. He knew it was only a matter of time before everything went back to normal. The parties would be rowdier and more explicit than ever before.

There was a time he'd loved the full-blown parties. After a long day, a hard week, or a bad month, there was nothing more satisfying than getting naked and fucking everything in sight.

He didn't think about the number of women he'd been with. Last year he'd gotten tested to make sure he was clean. He was clean and intended to stay that way. From the first moment he looked at Angel in town, Lash had known she was the woman for him.

She nibbled on her lip, and Lash remembered her lips wrapped around a straw. He couldn't stop it. Holding onto the back of her head, Lash smashed his lips against hers. Her hands moved to his chest, and Lash watched as she closed her eyes. When she did, he closed his own and allowed himself the pleasure of the kiss.

Angel moaned. He tilted her head back, nibbled on her lip and waited for her to open up to him. Her lips opened, and Lash took full advantage of it. Stroking his tongue into her mouth, Lash made love to her mouth. He fucked her mouth with his tongue, mimicking the movements he wanted to do between her thighs.

Her hands moved to his chest, gripping the fabric of his vest. Lash moved his hand down from her head to her back. He pushed her back to the bed until she was under him.

With careful movements, Lash settled between her thighs, and the denim skirt she wore rode up high around her waist. He stroked a hand up her thigh, feeling her silken skin against his palm.

Lash didn't press his cock against her centre. The only thing keeping him away from her was her panties and the denim of his jeans.

Making love to her mouth, Lash caressed her body as best as he could in the position. Her hands moved from his chest around to his back. Her nails sank into his shirt. If he'd been naked Lash would have her mark his back.

His cock was thick, and his need for her intensified.

"Kiss me back," he said, breaking the kiss long enough to speak.

Before she got chance to talk or push him away, Lash claimed her lips once again.

He fucked her mouth with his tongue and pressed his palm between them. Touching her pussy he felt her heat against him. Moaning, Lash kept her mouth occupied at the same time he pushed the fabric of her panties out of his way. He needed to touch her.

Slipping a finger through her folds, Lash touched her clit. She jumped under his touch. He kept her in place, sinking his fingers into her hair, holding her there.

Lash stroked her clit feeling her cream soak his fingers. She was so close, and Lash knew she'd never been touched like this before.

He fingered her clit, kissing her mouth and hoping he wasn't fucking up what was happening.

She cried out and seconds later shuddered under his touch. It was the most erotic experience of his life. Lash eased the touch of his fingers and then slowly withdrew from her heat.

Staring down into her face, Lash waited for her to open her eyes.

Angel looked at him, her face flushed from her orgasm. It hadn't taken long at all. He'd known it wouldn't.

"You're beautiful," he said. Without thinking he brought his fingers to his lips and sucked the cream from them.

She looked away from him, biting onto her lip.

"What did I just do?" she asked.

Her words were so faint that he only just heard them. "I suggest you get used to my touch, baby. I'm not going anywhere, and you're going to get used to my touch."

He pulled her to her feet and started to remove her clothing. All his planning left his thoughts. He'd wasted too long trying to take things slowly with Angel. She wasn't part of his world, but he'd make sure by the time he got his ring on her finger that she would be.

Lash was not going to hold back any longer. Angel was going to be claimed whether she liked it or not.

Pulling her shirt from her body, Lash tore at the denim skirt until she stood in her panties. Lash pulled his vest off. In the next instant he removed her bra and panties and then placed his vest over her head.

The vest fit perfectly and was a little tight around her large tits. They were *his* tits.

"What are you doing?" she asked.

He slammed his lips down on hers in answer. "Get in bed," he said.

She stared at him for a few minutes and then climbed into the bed.

Lash knelt beside her, took her hand and stared into her eyes. "Things are going to change for you. You're not always going to like me, and I accept that. I get what I want, and you'll do what I ask, and there's nothing that is going to change who I am. I'll do my best to make you happy, but from this day forward, you'll be my woman, Angel. No one will touch you but me."

He stroked her hair, kissed her cheek and left the room. Tiny was standing outside waiting for him. The leader of the club had his arms folded over his chest.

"I see you've finally decided to claim her," Tiny said.

"Yes." Lash turned to face his boss and waited for what Tiny had to say.

"Good. You claim her in front of the other men, and she'll be yours. Make sure you take care of her, Lash. I don't want her to be hurt."

Tiny didn't like to involve just anybody. They were a rough crew but a fair one all because of Tiny's influence. Yes, they ran the occasional coke deal, but it kept the drugs out of their town. Fort Wills was clean, and the folk had them to thank for that, not the cops. None of the crew used drugs either. Tiny made money out of it, and if he caught a member using, they were fucked.

"I'm taking full responsibility for her," Lash said.

"You better because her father is as good as dead. You need to be prepared for the fallout." Tiny slapped him on the back then left.

Resting against the door, Lash wondered how she was going to take the next couple of months. He wasn't waiting around anymore. Angel belonged to him, and the only person who didn't know that was Angel.

Chapter Three

Angel woke up early in the morning to banging on the door. She'd forgotten to set her alarm clock. Seconds later Lash walked in. Everything that happened last night came flooding back to her like a bad memory.

"Good morning," he said. He walked to the wardrobe, shook his head, and pulled out a pair of jeans. Her wardrobe was small. She hated clothes shopping and only ever bought what she thought was relevant to her.

"What are you doing here?" she asked, covering herself with the blanket. She wore his vest shirt and nothing else.

He'd brought her to orgasm, literally had his naked fingers on her pussy, and she was worried about him seeing her.

Last night was different. It had been dark last night, whereas it was now morning, and there was no chance for her to hide away from him. It was unfair and cruel.

"This is not acceptable at all." He turned to her and started tugging her out of bed.

"What are you doing?" she asked.

Lash wasn't answering her questions.

"We're going shopping, or I might send you out shopping with a Prospect. I've got shit to do."

Once she was dressed, without panties or a bra, Lash stood back to look at her.

"I think it will do for now."

"Wait, I need a bra and panties. I've never worn jeans without panties."

He took a step toward her. One hand sank into her hair, tugging on the length and the other rested between her thighs.

Angel was ashamed by the heat that consumed her from his touch. Would she ever *not* be affected by him?

Lash rubbed his hand back and forward creating a friction that almost brought her to her knees. Lash knew all the right buttons to press, and she hated him for it.

"No. Your tits look wonderful like that, and from now on I say what you wear."

Before she could protest his lips were once again on hers.

The kiss was brutal, all teeth and passion, and not once did Angel try to stop it. Finally, only when Lash was ready, did he break the kiss. Until he was ready, Lash was the one in control. She didn't have a say in what she wanted. It was all about what Lash wanted.

She didn't hate the thought either. Angel had never been good at making a decision or solving a problem. She was a waste of space.

"Don't put yourself down. Even when you're out of my presence I will know about it."

"How did you know I was doing that?" she asked. She should have argued his claim that she'd been putting herself down.

"I know you, baby. I know what you're thinking, and I see it in your eyes. You're like an open book. I can read everything by looking at you." His hand left her hair to grab her wrist. "Come on, it's breakfast downstairs."

"I know. I'm supposed to be the one getting the stuff."

"Not anymore. From now on your place is by my side or sat in my lap." He opened her bedroom door, and together they made their way toward the eating area. The eating area was the main part of the bar. All the tables had been pulled together to make a long table. The kitchen doors were thrown open showing several of the Prospects and the women getting ready to serve.

"Where the fuck is Angel? She's supposed to be doing this shit, not me," Fern asked. Fern was one of the women who got passed around from member to member. Angel had seen her with a different guy every night. From what she heard none of the men wanted to claim her. She was a sweet-butt whose sole purpose was to open her legs for whoever wanted her.

Angel would hate that kind of existence, but some women seemed to love it.

The room went silent as The Skulls noticed Lash and her together. She felt their gazes on her skin and saw them look at her face before looking at Lash's shirt.

"It looks like you better get used to being in the kitchen, sweet-butt. Angel has been taken," Zero said.

"What?" Fern stormed out of the kitchen, and Angel watched her stop when she looked at her.

"Oh hell no. That is not fair. She hasn't even been a member or done the time or the fucking the rest of us have. What does she have that the rest of us don't?" Her hands were on her hips, and the look Fern shot Lash would have killed him if looks could kill.

"Lash made a choice. We accepted that choice, and she stays," Tiny said. He sat at the top of the table with his hands locked together. The leader looked calm and frightening. Tiny always scared Angel. Her grip tightened on Lash's hand.

"You've got to wait until someone actually wants your sweet ass, baby," Nash said.

Angel glanced at Lash's brother and saw the contempt the other man had for Fern. Most of the men loved to fuck her, but none of them liked her.

"Whatever." Fern sent her a glare then stormed back into the kitchen.

Lash took a seat next to his brother. She made to go to the kitchen, but the hand around her wrist stopped her.

"I need to go and help," she said.

"You're not helping. Sit the fuck down and wait."

Arguing with him was not an option. Glancing around the table, Angel couldn't see any available chairs free.

With one quick tug, Lash had her on his lap. She felt the hard ridge of his cock, and she tried her best to ignore it, even as heat filled her cheeks. There was no way for her to ignore Lash. He was too large, and from the feel of his shaft against her ass, he was big everywhere.

Two cups of coffee were placed in front of her. Angel recognised Tate, Tiny's daughter, as she placed the cup in front of her. The younger woman rarely came to the club, but when she did the crew were always on their best behaviour. Tiny didn't like bad shit happening around his girl. Tate was older than Angel by a couple of years.

"It's nice to see one of the men treating you nice," Tate said.

Angel smiled at her not knowing what to say. Tate was like her, thicker than the other girls in the club. Angel once heard that the men preferred thin women and hated old ladies who got fat.

If that was the case what was Lash doing with her?

She sat on his lap, and Lash grabbed a newspaper. Everything felt surreal to her. She was sat on Lash's lap, reading a newspaper while being waited on.

"We got a lot of work to do today, boys. I expect you all to be out to the warehouse for our meeting. No women, no old ladies, only yourself and your bike," Tiny said.

Fern walked back to the table, slamming down plates and glaring at her.

Angel stayed still not wanting to draw any unnecessary attention.

"Come on, man. When are we going to have a proper fucking party? I need to get laid by real sluts," Butch said.

"Shut your mouth, Butch, otherwise I'll make sure you don't see any action for months," Tiny said.

Angel saw him looking at his daughter as he spoke.

Butch's mouth stayed closed while Tate placed food in front of Tiny and then moved back to the kitchen.

"Sorry."

"When Tate's here, you stay quiet." Tiny spoke while cutting into his breakfast.

No member used his real name. She knew Tiny either picked names out, or members chose their own names. From what she heard, Tiny's name was chosen by his late wife.

When Tate brought her breakfast through, she saw it was on one plate and was handed to Lash.

"I'm the one who gets to feed you."

"Move," Tate said. Angel turned to see the other woman was speaking to Nash.

"Why do I have to move?"

"Because I said."

Lash chuckled. "Come on, brother, you know she'll get what she wants."

His brother moved leaving room for Tate to sit next to them. "It's archaic making her eat from your fingers, Lash."

"Only because you've never found a man strong enough to stand up to your father."

"That's the truth. None of these men will have the guts to stand up to Dad and make a play for me. In fact none of the men in Fort Wills will touch me." Tate let out a sigh and started eating.

Angel stared at the other woman in sympathy.

"I'm sending a Prospect with Angel today. She needs new clothes, and I've not got the time to go with her," Lash said, half-way through breakfast.

"I'll go as well. I need new shoes," Tate said, speaking up.

Around her people organised her day, and Angel was left no choice other than to do what they asked.
****

Lash stood with his brother and Tiny. They'd gone through the three Prospects they had and come to Prospect Steven. He was twenty years old, skinny but could fight. From what Lash knew of him, he was a good kid and loyal to the club.

"You're on babysitting duty. Anything happens to the girls it's on your head," Tiny said.

He counted off some notes and handed them to Steven. Lash did the same.

"Whatever Tate wants, you get it her. I don't want to hear her moaning or anything." Tiny gave some more instructions and then left Steven to him.

Lash handed over plenty of cash. "I want good, designer shops. None of the shitty thrift stories they have. Make sure you take them to the mall out of town, and if you do, you pack your stuff. There's plenty of action from other crews. If you see other tags you get out of there."

"I've got it. Take the girls shopping, make sure they spend a shit load of cash, and keep them safe,"

Steven said. "I'll keep an eye on them. Both of them will be safe with me. I promise."

"Good." Lash slapped the Prospect on the shoulder and moved toward his woman. Angel was stood near the door, her arms folded while Tate did nothing but talk. Tate clearly liked his woman.

"Here comes trouble," Tate said.

Angel looked, and he was caught in her green gaze. Going to her side, he pushed the hair from her face and looked down into her eyes. "You're to have fun today. I've given the money to Steven, and I should be back this afternoon."

"You don't have to pay for anything."

"My woman, my rules, Angel." He pressed his lips against hers. "See you later, and be good."

Before he left the club he made sure Steven knew to get her a cell phone. He wanted to be in touch with her at all times. Nash stayed silent behind him as he instructed Steven. There were only a few years between them as brothers.

"Man, you've got it bad," Nash said.

They stood by their bikes on the forecourt of the club.

Each of the men was saying bye to their ladies or the women who satisfied their needs.

"I've always had it bad for Angel."

"I know, but this is different and you know it. You're the reason Tiny called in the debt and the reason David is not dead yet," Nash said.

"There are times I wish you weren't my brother."

"Yeah, having someone know everything about you must suck. Does Angel know the extent of your obsession?"

Lash glanced back at the club in time to see Tate talking with Angel as they left the building. She glanced over toward him but didn't do anything else. Steven climbed into the car with the two women going in the back.

"No, she doesn't have a clue what I've done to keep her safe and to keep her for myself." Since the moment she turned eighteen, Lash had done everything he could to keep her safe and to keep the problems her father brought to their life, away from her.

Steven pulled out of the parking lot, and Lash turned his attention back to his brother. "And you're not going to tell her. Angel doesn't need to know everything, and I'll tell her what I think she needs to know when I'm good and ready."

He put the helmet on and flung his leg over the bike, straddling the machine.

"You better. I've heard shit like this has a tendency to blow up in your face."

"I don't intend to have anything blow up in my face. It's going to work."

Tiny pulled out onto the main road, and everyone else followed suit. The two remaining Prospects stayed behind with the others.

Riding on his bike, Lash followed the rest of the crew through town and out onto the main road. They needed to travel a good hour to get to the warehouse that stored most of their business.

It had once been a boxing factory, but when the recession hit, the factory went under and plenty of people lost their jobs. The club had banded together and laid claim to it. None of the old ladies ever visited the warehouse, and no one who wasn't part of the club came close to the warehouse, not even the law. Since the death of Lash's and Nash's parents over turf, Tiny had done everything he could to make the town safe. No club deals went down near town, and no other crew came to Fort Wills.

The ride was a long one, but it allowed Lash time to clear his head. There were times he struggled to think when he was right in the middle of a problem. Riding his bike gave him the freedom and the quiet to think of every problem.

Angel was not a problem, but her father was. He hadn't been joking when he'd told her David wouldn't make it to the end of the year. The Skulls were trying to regroup their losses caused by David. Other than get back some money, the rest of the club wanted him dead. Lash had asked for a little more time. If they took David out of the equation too soon, Lash would lose any chance he had with Angel.

Time was not on his side. It wouldn't be long before the club voted against David being gone. The older man was stalling too damn much and making it hard to believe his stories. The guy was full of it. The death of Angel's mom had left David broken in some way. Whatever the reason, it wasn't something the club took into consideration.

By the time he pulled up outside the warehouse Lash wasn't any clearer as to what he wanted. Climbing off the bike, he lit a cigarette and waited for Nash and the others to pull up the rear.

"Whoo," Nash said, laughing. "There's nothing like a ride to put the air in your lungs."

There was a bolt across the door along with several locks in place to keep people out.

"I know what you mean." Taking a long pull on his cigarette, Lash looked up at the sky. It was a hot, clear day, and his thoughts returned to Angel. He wondered if she was having fun. Tate was an amazing girl. She'd been a little toddler when Tiny took him and Nash into the fold. His old lady was still alive back then. Pain struck whenever he thought about Tiny's woman, who'd been like a mother to him. Patricia cared for everyone, and Tiny was her whole world. It was watching and listening to the pair that made Lash know he'd never have a sweet-butt for a wife. Patricia had been an outsider, but her love for Tiny kept her by his side. Her death hit their leader hard, but Tiny finally worked his way out of the heartache. Tate was like Patricia in a lot of ways. Tiny wouldn't let her get involved in the club even though the younger woman wanted to.

"Thinking about Patricia?" Nash asked.

"Yeah, she was the one who suggested this place to Tiny." Lash looked at the warehouse. How Tiny still made it through the doors was beyond him. He couldn't imagine losing anything so precious to him. If something was to happen to Angel, he couldn't even breathe at the thought let alone live with it. There was never going to be a way for him to live with it.

"I miss her, too. She was a strong woman. I could never allow myself to love someone that much and then watch her die."

"Is that why you fuck and take blow jobs from women you won't keep?" Lash asked.

"It saves being alone and in pain." Nash slapped him on the shoulder. "Come on, let's go so you can get your pansy fucking ass back to Angel."

Together they walked into the warehouse.

David was sat at a desk typing away at the computer. Several other members of The Skulls were stood around the warehouse. They all took turns in babysitting David. When they left, whoever stayed behind was locked inside the warehouse until the next morning.

Lash had spent two nights with the bastard, listening to him mutter on about his wife and daughter. He didn't like the older man, but he was his woman's father. Lash had no choice but to try to help him out.

"Give us some good news, David. I'm growing tired of this shit, and your daughter's ass is looking tempting," Tiny said.

Fisting his hands at his side, Lash knew there was nothing sinister in what Tiny said, but hearing the words was still hard to handle. The civilians didn't need to know that The Skulls had a code. If Lash hadn't laid claim to her to all the members, Angel would have been fucked within her first week at the club.

They didn't run a hotel service, and the men needed a regular supply of sex in whatever form that came.

"I-I-I can't g-g-get i-i-it back."

Rolling his eyes, Lash saw through the lies.

"Then I guess Angel's ass is mine."

"No!"

The shout was firm. David might be an asshole, but he didn't want anything to happen to his daughter.

For the next two hours Lash listened to the man talk shit about the money. Lash and Nash were brothers, and together they'd worked out the holes in David's stories. They knew where the money was and how to get it. All The Skulls wanted to know was which side David was on.

LASH

Chapter Four

Angel waited outside of the dressing room while Tate tried on another item of clothing. Steven stood several feet away from them, but his eyes never left where they both stood. She'd purchased some designer jeans and a few tops all at Steven's request. He'd mumbled something to Tate, and from then on the other woman took control so that Angel now possessed clothes she would never even dream of buying, let alone wearing. There were several dresses she didn't think were legal to wear in town.

"Ta-da," Tate said, opening the dressing room door. The other woman wore a tight red dress. "How do I look?" The dress moulded to every curve and highlighted the other woman's fuller figure.

"You look amazing."

"Do you really think so?" Tate asked. Her hands moved down her sides to rest on her hips.

"There's only one problem," Angel said.

"What is it?"

"Where are you going to wear it? It's a beautiful dress, but where could you wear something like that?" Angel glanced down at her clasped hands. She'd never been good at this. Girly shopping trips and bonding trips were never her thing.

"Haven't you heard of some of the parties the club has?" Tate asked, taking a seat beside Angel.

"Yeah, I've seen them."

"No, honey, you've seen the tame ones. If you speak to the other old ladies you'd have a clue as to what goes on at these parties. There's a lot more risqué shit going down. My Dad tries to keep me all sweet and innocent, but let me tell you I'm not stupid."

Angel listened to the other woman speak and knew in her heart that Tate spoke the truth. If the parties they'd been having were not the real deal then no wonder the men hated her. Was she the reason the parties had been downgraded?

"Tiny's your Dad. What makes you think he's even going to let you attend one of these things?" Angel asked.

"When I walk through the door he won't stop me. Dad needs to know I'm a grown up and stop scaring guys away from me. If I don't act now I'm going to die a virgin, and that's pitiful." Tate grabbed her hand. "The other girls are horrid. They only put up with me because of my Dad. You're different. I can see that. Also, you're not horribly underweight either."

Tate wrapped her arms around Angel.

"I don't know what to say."

Angel looked over at Steven to see him pressing on a load of buttons on his cell phone.

The sound of the door opening, followed by some giggling and screaming, made Tate pause in her tracks. Angel glanced over to see what all the fuss was about.

"We've got to go," Steven said, helping them with their bags.

"Shit, it's the Lions," Tate said, muttering under her breath.

"Who are the Lions?" Angel asked. She saw the women and men in leather jackets sporting the Lion emblem.

"They're The Skulls' biggest problem, and we're in neutral ground. The cities are not claimed." Tate made to go to the changing room.

"We're paying for it with you in the dress, Tate."

"I need to get changed."

"I've got orders from Tiny to get you back to the club. We're paying for you in it."

Tate didn't look afraid as they passed the other crews path. All of them stopped with Steven standing in front of them.

A dark haired man stopped to look at Tate. His gaze wandered up and down her body. The heat coming from his eyes couldn't be mistaken as anything other than predatory.

"Tate, it's lovely to see you again."

"Murphy, what brings you here?"

Angel stayed quiet, watching the interaction.

"Shopping," Murphy said.

"For the skanks of the Lions. I see that. It mustn't cost you too much. From the looks of them you don't really need to keep them in clothing."

"Tate," Angel said, grabbing her new friend's arm.

"Not right now, I've got this." Tate didn't turn her attention away from the man in front of her.

"You're not going to let her speak to us like that?" one of the woman said.

Angel didn't know who spoke, but Murphy and Tate kept glaring at each other.

"She's Tiny's girl. Tate says what she wants and does what she wants," Murphy said, seconds later.

"Exactly, and what Tate wants is to get out of here. Lions give everything a bad press."

Angel followed Tate and Steven to the checkout counter. She glanced behind her to see Murphy watching Tate.

None of them said a word while Tate got the women to scan the dress while it was still on her body.

Once they were out of the store, Tate refused to go home. Angel stood waiting while Tate ranted over the cell with her father.

Angel kept looking at Steven, whose attention drifted between Tate and the designer shop they'd come from.

"Do you know what happened in there?" Angel asked.

"I don't know, and I don't make it my business to know. The Lions are a threat, and my only job is to keep you two safe."

Angel nodded not wanting to press him for any more details.

Tate returned several seconds later. "I won. We can shop for a few more hours."

Neither of them waited for Steven. Tate took the lead and moved toward the next shop. Together they picked out a dress and headed toward the dressing room.

"What was that about, Tate?" Angel asked. Her curiosity was getting the better of her.

"What was what?"

"You know, between you and that Murphy guy?" Angel tugged Lash's shirt over her head and waited for the other woman to speak. Tate let out a sigh, which she heard between the changing room.

"Murphy is an ass who joined the Lions because he thought The Skulls were too hard. He's a backstabbing asshole who can't be trusted."

She heard the pain in Tate's voice.

"Did you and he have a thing?"

Silence met her answer. Angel finished changing into the tight black dress and cringed when she looked in the mirror. She looked like an overweight whale.

"He was the only one who dared to have anything to do with me. He's older than I am, but there was a time when I thought he was sweet. Murphy taught me not to let go so easily. I'm not looking for a boyfriend or a husband, Angel. I'm just looking for a man to help ease the loneliness." The curtain opened, and Tate stood in a full blue gown. "I know we've never been close and I'm a few years older than you, but in time we'll get to know each other. I do want to be your friend and share everything with you. For now, I don't want to talk about it anymore, okay?"

"Okay."

Angel smiled, distracting the other woman. "I think I look like a whale. What do you think?" She gave a little twirl in the hope of breaking any tension.

"You don't look like a whale, and Lash is going to get a hard-on when he looks at you. You're such a beautiful woman."

The rest of the day was spent shopping, and by the late afternoon, Angel was tired and wishing for a break. They ate burgers at the takeout place. The Lions took a seat across from them. Angel noticed Murphy watching Tate the whole time. Steven kept texting on his cell phone. The whole experience was tense, and by the end Angel was thankful to leave.

During the drive home everyone was quiet. The bikes were parked on the forecourt outside the club. Tate didn't make a move to get out of the car.

"Are you coming in?" Angel asked.

"No, Dad is taking me back home. Steven is going to give him a rundown of everything that happened, and then he'll help you with your bags. I'll see you tomorrow. I'm not letting my Dad keep me away."

Angel nodded and turned to get out of the car. Before she left, Tate pulled her in tight for a hug.

"I'm sorry for being a bitch. I don't like opening up, and it can be hard at times."

"Don't worry about it. You don't need to be open with me. Take care, and I hope you're feeling happy again soon," Angel smiled at the other woman then made to leave.

"You really don't hold a grudge against anyone, do you?" Tate asked.

"Not if I can help it."

"Okay, you're really special. Lash is not the best guy in the world, but he'll treat you right." Tate glanced over her shoulder. "Speak of the devil."

Angel looked over to see Lash coming out of the building. He stopped to talk with Tiny and Steven. All the time his gaze was on her.

Glancing down at the floor, Angel did everything she could to compose herself.

"Good luck with him. He's going to be a handful."

"Nash!" The word was shouted from Lash's lips. His brother appeared with a smile.

"What's the matter? Why are you yelling?" Nash asked.

"Help me load up Angel's purchases. She's going home with me tonight."

"What about the rules?"

"Tiny, do you have problem with me taking Angel home?"

"No, do what you need to do, son," Tiny said.

In no time at all, her bags were moved to the trunk of a car, and she was placed in the front beside Lash. No words were spoken between them. Nash waved at them before they were pulling out of the parking lot.

"I heard what happened at the mall," Lash said.

"Nothing really happened. There was a standoff between Murphy and Tate, but nothing else happened. I don't really know what went on, only that something did."

"Murphy hurt Tate a long time ago. The Lions are our biggest problem at the moment. They're fighting for turf and for a chance to get into Fort Wills. Tiny's not having any of it."

Angel sat beside Lash and wondered what the hell was going on between them.

"Did you see my father today?" she asked.

"Yes."

He didn't elaborate any further.

"Where are we going?"

"To my house."

****

Lash didn't speak anymore on her father because they'd left the man with a black eye and a couple of bruises along his body. The bastard was playing them for fools, and Lash didn't like it. When the call had come through from Steven, he'd been ready to kill David. The Lions were their biggest enemy, and Murphy posed a threat just as much as the whole crew, what with being in the position he was in. No one in The Skulls talked about Murphy. It was better not to.

The Skulls lived by their code, and they didn't let anyone break it. If they broke any of the rules then they dealt with the club and not in a good way. They were strict on several things, including the age of the girls who came in as old ladies and even as the girls they screwed with no intention of making it more. Eighteen was the limit for all women and men. They didn't interfere in members' relationships, and they didn't sleep with each other's women. If the woman in question slept with another member beforehand that was the risk guys took. Lash didn't want any other woman that the guys had been inside.

They never hurt children. They drank but never did drugs even though they distributed outside of town, and everything else was their own rules. The club partied hard, were rough and did whatever the hell they wanted, but they lived by their own set of rules. They were not controlled by the rules society gave them but what they gave themselves.

The Lions, however, didn't have a code, and Lash was repulsed by them. He didn't even want to think about what they would do to his woman if given the chance.

"Why are we going to your house?"

"It's where you're staying tonight. We'll go back to the club, but I needed to get out of there before I did something I would regret. Nash is staying there, so we don't have to worry about being disturbed."

She was quiet, and he glanced over in her direction in time to see her frowning. He knew he was moving too fast for her, but it was something he needed to do. If he didn't bombard her with attention, Angel would find some way to stay away from him. He wasn't going to let that happen. They drove away from town, through the forest toward his secluded home. Lash had bought the plot two years ago and spent most of his spare time doing up the house on it. He'd always wanted something what his parents shared. Before they'd been killed his parents had given him and Nash a perfect home. Their father had been part of The Skulls, but he'd made sure they had a normal family life. Lash couldn't recall if his mother hated the lifestyle.

"This is your house?" Angel asked.

"Yeah, this is my baby." He turned the engine off and climbed out of the car.

He went to the trunk of the car, opened it up, and started gathering the bags she'd bought.

"I look forward to seeing you in these," Lash said.

He saw her blush, but she nodded.

Lash made his way to the front door. He pulled out his key, unlocked the three locks before the door opened. Safety was a key issue for him, and he'd designed all three locks only to be open by his one key. Fort Wills was a safe place, but the club wasn't. He could be the target for others at any time.

Angel didn't say anything, and for that he was thankful. He couldn't handle lying to her right now. After the fear of learning the Lions were close to her, Lash had been ready to murder.

The sun was setting, but it provided enough light for him to dump the packages on the table and floor and go straight for the fridge.

"Okay, wow, did you decorate your home with someone in mind?" Angel asked, looking around her.

"What do you mean?"

"Why do you even stay in the club? This place is amazing." She folded her arms smiling all around her.

He'd decorated his kitchen without any expense to be spared.

"Do you like it?" he asked.

"Like it, I love it. You've got a keen eye, Lash."

It was the most she'd ever spoken, and she seemed to stop and take a breath. He hated the sight of watching her deflate.

She took a seat and stared at her linked hands.

"Why are you withdrawing from me?" He pulled out a beer and a bottle of orange juice. Popping the lids off the top he walked over to the table. Pushing the clothes out of the way, he handed her the orange before taking a sip of his drink.

"What is this? I mean, up until last night I didn't even know you knew my name, and now I'm wearing your shirt, sitting in your dining room, and I don't understand." She wouldn't look at him. "And last night, you ..."

She didn't finish. Her checks were a wonderful shade of pink from her blush. Reaching out, he stroked the pads of his fingers along her cheek.

"Last night I touched your sweet pussy and made you come. I've staked my claim on you, Angel. As far as the club is concerned you're my woman, and there's nothing else to it. You're mine, you'll always be mine, and I'll do everything in my power to protect you."

Angel shook her head. "No, this is not right. I'm the daughter of a guy who can't pay you back. I was taken as payment."

She placed the bottle on the counter and didn't reach out to touch it again.

"And you're still there as payment, Angel. Nothing has changed other than the fact the guys know to stay away."

Her mouth opened and then closed. "What?"

"Your father is never going to pay back the money, baby. He's in too deep, and we think he's into something deeper. The longer we go without being paid, the higher the risk of you being one of the members' plaything, rises." The look of disgust made him feel like a pig. Angel was far too innocent. Why couldn't he want a woman who knew how things went with him?

"You're telling me they'd treat me like some kind of whore?"

"No. You're a challenge to the men."

"My virginity is a challenge to them?" She let out a gross sound. "Well I'm sorry, okay. I'm sorry that my Dad had to borrow money, and I'm sorry my Mom died sending him to do it. I've got nothing to do with it. Why can't you just leave me alone?" She stood up and made toward the door.

Lash fought with himself. He should just let her go and help her get far away from The Skulls and him. She'd be safer without him being close by. Instead, he found himself getting to his feet and charging in her direction. She was stood in front of the door leading to her escape.

He couldn't let her go. Tiny would kill him, and the club would look down on him. He either tamed her or got rid of her. They were a club with a code, but the club would always come first, even to him.

Slamming the door closed, he stopped her from moving. Her head rested against the door, and he felt the sobs escape her. Her shoulder shook with her tears.

"Why can't I just go? I've never done anything to any of you." The pain in her voice was clear.

"I can't."

"I'm not used to this. I don't watch people having sex in front of an audience. I don't cook for a bunch of tattooed bikers. This is not me. It's not fair."

He pulled her hair off her shoulder and laid a kiss to her exposed flesh. "I know, and I'm sorry."

She shook her head. "No, you're not sorry. If you were sorry you'd let me go."

"There's no way you're leaving, Angel. You're my woman. You stay by my side."

"I hate you. I don't know you, but I hate you. You're unfair, and I hate you for it."

Lash listened to her words and reached around to cup her breast. Her nipple hardened in his palm. He didn't let up from his touch.

With his other hand he pulled the vest he'd given her up over her chest until he was touching her naked tit in his palm. She filled his hand with her nipple poking against him.

"You can hate me all you want, baby. Your body doesn't lie, and you want me. Hate me all you want, but you're mine. Your body is mine, and I'll be fucking you very soon."

Dropping his lips against her neck Lash inhaled her subtle fragrance. Her scent was addictive, and he wanted to surround himself with her scent.

She let out a moan, and her hands lay flat against the door. He wasn't letting her get away.

"I can't do this."

"Yes, you can." He dropped one of his hands to her jeans and flicked open the button of her jeans. She didn't fight him. His Angel didn't stop him when he slipped his hand inside her jeans and through her creamy slit. Her pussy was dripping wet and coated his palm with her cream.

Their moans combined and floated away in the air. He nibbled her neck relishing the feel of her against him.

Chapter Five

Angel wanted to fight him, but no matter how much she tried a new wave of pleasure consumed her, stopping her from putting an end to Lash's touch. Did she really want him to stop? Fingers stroked over her clit, and Angel was lost to anything other than the sensation he was creating.

"You're so slippery. Hate me, baby. I can handle the hate. I see it in the faces of people in town, but your body will always want me. I can make you feel so good. You know that, and so do I."

She didn't fight him as he turned her around to face him. Her back against the door, she watched him kneel down before her. Lash removed the jeans from her body, exposing her to his gaze.

His eyes never once left her face. He opened her thighs, and only then did his gaze wander down her body. She wanted to cover her fuller figure. Her thighs were thick, and she was sure they had a few dots of cellulite. Lash gripped her thighs, firmly. He split open her body for him to look.

Angel stared at his head and felt his fingers open her pussy.

"You're going to have to get this waxed. I want my woman to be bare. I don't want any restriction in getting to you."

There was no way she was going to get her pubic hair waxed. The thought alone made her feel sick. The sickness was soon replaced by his very expert tongue.

Crying out, Angel gazed down in time to see his tongue circle her clit and then suck the whole nub into his mouth. She couldn't breathe. Hands flat behind her, Angel did everything she could to keep herself upright.

His hands moved from her pussy lips to grip her ass.

"I'll hold you steady, baby, open your lips for me. I want you to offer your pussy to me."

She shook her head. There was no way she'd open herself up to him. It was madness. It would be sheer madness to become vulnerable to him.

Still, she reached down between their bodies and opened her pussy for him to devour. When it came to Lash she didn't have any control.

What's wrong with me?

"That's it, baby. Give me what I want."

This tattoo-covered biker was making her lose control, and she hated it. For most of her teenage years she'd always imagined being with a guy who was like her. Who would be happy to stay out of the Fort Wills business and to have a small family and earn enough to support themselves.

She never thought she'd be considering giving her virginity to a guy who'd probably been with hundreds of girls.

His tongue was pure sin. She couldn't get past how amazing it felt having his tongue on her body. He licked, nibbled, and sucked at her clit. She felt his tongue glide over her fingers before smashing against her clit.

"Come for me, Angel." He muttered the words against her flesh.

"I can't."

"Yes, you can."

His hand tightened on her ass stopping her from arguing.

"Come for me now, or I'll take you over my knee and slap your ass."

The threat registered at the same time as his grip tightened even further on her ass. She knew there was going to be bruising. Closing her eyes Angel stopped thinking about everything that could happen and should have happened in her future. She thought about Lash and how sexy he was. The scar down the left side of his face pulled her in, grabbing her attention. She wanted to caress his face and see if the scar was rough or soft. His dark hair was thick and fell around his head and looked messy. On Lash, his hair fit. He was so tall that he made her feel small, delicate almost. She wasn't used to being delicate. Being a larger woman meant she always felt like a beached whale. His hands were twice the size of hers, and his muscles made her mouth water.

He was the complete opposite of everything she thought she wanted. Lash was relentless, and the feel of his tongue against her clit was too much.

Keeping the lips of her pussy open, Angel felt the first stirrings of her orgasm. She trusted Lash to hold her up. The grip on her ass was firm. He wasn't going to let her go.

She cried out, the sound echoing around the room as she finally let go. Wave upon wave of pleasure engulfed her. She shuddered and heard Lash slurp the cream leaking from her body.

Her embarrassment was complete. The orgasm died away, and he pulled away. She saw his chin glisten in the small light.

"You're so fucking tasty. I can't wait to lick you again and again."

He stood and claimed her lips, slipping his tongue into her mouth. She tasted herself on his lips and tried to push him away. The instant her hands touched his hard shoulders the chance for pushing him away was lost.

Hands sank into her hair, tugging on the length until she was pulled up taut against him.

Lash took charge, moving her away from the door and back through to the dining room. All the time his lips never once left hers. He threw the clothes off the hard surface of the table without breaking contact. She had no clue how he managed to get her partially naked and flat on a table, but he did. The fight she originally had left her in light of what they were doing to each other.

He lifted her onto the table, opening her thighs wide.

"I can't get e-fucking-nough of you. I want you so bad. My balls and cock ache." He kissed a path down her neck to her collarbone. Lash didn't stop there. He tore his vest in two exposing her chest to his view.

"So fucking sexy. I can't wait to see these tits bouncing around in front of me." Lash pinched one nipple and then the other.

Angel was completely naked, and from the pleasure alone, she didn't care.

He stepped back, removed his jacket and shirt until he stood in front of her naked. She got a clear shot of the snake tattoo on his arm and the love heart over his chest. On his hip was a small picture of a tree and lines where names needed to go.

She watched, unable to tear her gaze away, when he tore at his jeans until they were thrown to the floor. His boots were taken off during the undressing. She also got a shot of a tattoo on his back, a picture of a skull and cross-bones with the titles Fort Wills and The Skulls across the top and underneath.

Lash turned back to her butt ass naked. His cock stood out long, thick, and proud. She saw the tip leaking pre-cum, which he smeared over the head. He was that aroused his foreskin was pulled away, exposing the mushroomed tip.

It was her first real look at him. His body was twice the size of hers but without a trace of fat visible. She doubted he even had a blob of cellulite.

"I'm not ready," she said, holding up her hands when he came closer.

"I'm not going to fuck you like this. We can do a lot more than fuck. Besides, your first time is not going to be on my fucking dining room table." He came over, settling between her thighs.

What could they possibly do?

He teased the tip of his cock through her slit. She gazed down to see the thick rod of his shaft laid between her pussy lips. Her cream coated the length making it slippery.

"This is insane. What are you doing?" she asked.

Lash smirked. "I've made you come twice. I think it's my time."

"Excuse me?"

"I'm getting off, baby. I need release, and I'm not finding any other woman to give me what I want. It's only you."

He shut her up with his mouth. She felt him get harder through the slit of her pussy. During his kiss, Lash started to move against her. With each thrust of his hips Lash bumped her clit, making her cry out.

When her mouth opened, Lash slammed his tongue deep inside.

There was nothing for her to do other than stroke him with her own. They made love on top of his dining room table without him once entering her. Angel got closer to orgasm with each caress of her clit.

His dick was thick and large. She didn't know if he'd be able to fit inside her and was pleased they weren't going to try tonight. He started to pant, and his tongue thrust into her, harder and faster than ever before.

"Come for me, Angel. I want to feel you come again."

She gave him what he wanted. There was no stopping the way she felt. The pent up of emotion was too much. She reached climax within a matter of moments. Seconds later Lash thrust against her one final time, and then she felt the spurts of his seed as they landed on her stomach.

He let out a male growl and shuddered.

Angel stared up at him, unsure what to do. He looked in pain. She touched him arm trying to gain his attention. His eyes opened, and she was caught in their intense blue stare.

"Are you all right?" she asked.

"I should be asking you that question."

She frowned at him.

"You've never had a guy spunk on you, baby. This is a lot of firsts with you. How are you handling it?" he asked.

First, she hated the word spunk. It was crass and one of the worst things she'd ever heard. Many of the guys at the club shouted it or spoke about it. Other than that, she'd loved everything he'd done to her body. Licking her lips, she stared up at him wishing there was something she could say. Complaining about his use of the word spunk was petty. She wouldn't bring it up. Lash was harder and rougher by choice. She needed to accept that about him.

"I'm handling everything fine." She nodded her head. Her insides were all tied in knots. She didn't know how to handle what was happening. Twenty-four hours ago she hadn't been touched by anyone, and now she was being wet humped on a dining room table. Angel couldn't think what to call it. She knew it wasn't dry humping and feeling how wet she was, it was the only way she could describe it. They'd wet humped on the table, and now her stomach was covered with his semen.

Totally strange turn of events considering she didn't think Lash knew she existed. She'd been wrong.

****

Only with great restraint did Lash pull away from her body. How he managed to hump her pussy without fucking it was beyond him. Staring down at her stomach he saw the droplets of his seed coating her skin. A primal part of him wanted to rub the sticky seed into her skin. He wanted to mark her body and skin so every man knew who she belonged to.

He moved away long enough to grab a towel. When she made to move off the table, Lash stopped her with a hand to her stomach.

"What are you doing?" she asked.

"I'm going to admire my pussy." Lash reached down, grabbing his cigarettes and a lighter. Grabbing the seat he'd pushed to the floor, he righted it and took a seat.

She was shaking as he turned to fully look at her body. He lit up a cigarette, inhaled the nicotine before breathing it out. Lash knew he needed to quit. There was no way he'd make Angel kiss him with smoker's breath. He needed the smoke after the restraint he'd just shown.

"Smoking will kill you, you know?" she said.

Lash laughed. "I know, baby. After the orgasm you've just given me, I need a little reprieve."

He heard her giggle, and the sound was delightful to him.

"How old are you?" she asked, catching him by surprise.

"What?"

"I don't even know how old you are. Is that bad?"

Taking another deep draw on his cigarette Lash returned his gaze to her creamy pussy. Her clit was still swollen, and her lips were soaking wet from her cream. He'd wiped most of the semen away, but he wished it covered her pussy.

He looked forward to her getting a wax down there. Lash would be able to lick, suck, and nibble on her lips, clit and pussy all day long.

"It's bad for anyone else. You don't know a lot about me. I'm twenty-nine, baby." He flicked ash in the ash tray and continued to stare at her cunt.

His cock thickened from the sight alone.

With his free hand, he started to pump the flesh.

"Do you know how old I am?" Angel asked. Her voice was small.

He chanced a glance in her direction to see her staring up at the ceiling.

"I know how old you are." He waited a few minutes to see if she'd ask. "You're nineteen years old, and your favourite colour is blue."

Lash hated the fact he knew so much about her. His knowledge of her made him feel like a stalker.

"I can't believe this is happening," she said.

He laughed, finished his cigarette and removed the ashtray from view. Lash moved to the sink, washed his hands and walked to her side.

"What don't you believe?" Helping her off the table, Lash waited for her to elaborate.

"You must think I'm completely weird."

Shaking his head, Lash bent down to pick up some bags. "I don't think you're weird. Don't put any clothes on and follow me."

He headed up the stairs. Going straight for the main bedroom he opened the door and deposited the bags on the bed. "This is our room." Moving toward a closet Lash opened the door. His clothes were on one side of the walk-in-wardrobe. "Put your new shit here. The stuff you've got at the club is being burned. I don't want to see you in anything but what I paid for."

Leaving her to start on her clothes, Lash collected the other bags, put them on the bed then moved toward the bathroom. He quickly brushed his teeth and then walked back to the bedroom.

Angel was sorting through the bags, her body gloriously naked to his gaze.

"You follow instructions well."

"I've not got any other choice."

He frowned when he heard the wobble in her voice.

"Excuse me?"

She glanced up at him. "I've heard several rumours that we either do as you say or you get angry and hurt people."

Hands fisted at his side, Lash stared at her and knew it wasn't her fault for listening to the rumours. "I would never hurt you, Angel. You've got a choice here. I'm not going to force you to be with me."

She dropped her head, and he couldn't stand the thought of her thinking of him any differently.

Going to her, he dropped to his knees beside her and took her chin in his hands. He forced her to look at him. He stared into her green eyes and knew he'd do everything in his power to make her happy.

"I would never try anything with you that you wouldn't enjoy. I'm a lot of things, Angel, but I'm not a molester or a rapist."

"I know that." She pulled out of his touch and stood. He followed her into the wardrobe as she placed the next item on the rail. "I know you're not like that."

He stopped her from moving by blocking her path. "Look at me."

She tilted her head back to stare at him.

"Tell me you wanted me to do those things to you."

Lash needed for her to say the words. "Please don't make me say it."

"I've never taken a woman against her will. I don't intend to start now. You tell me you wanted it, or I swear to God, I will send you back to the club and I'll never touch you again."

It would kill him to do that, but he'd make sure Tiny protected her.

"Yes."

Her voice was so silent that he didn't hear her clearly.

"What?"

"Yes, I liked everything you did to me. It was nice. More than nice, and I don't think you'd make me do something I wouldn't enjoy."

Her cheeks were bright red, but he believed her words. For now, her word would do. She was a virgin. He planned to rectify that, but for now he was happy with what they were doing to each other.

"Finish putting your shit away. I'll expect to see everything on you at some point. I'm going to get some chicken in the oven for dinner. When you're done we'll shower together."

He dropped a kiss to her lips before leaving the bedroom. Heading down to the kitchen, he pulled the chicken from the fridge and started arranging it in a meat tray. He drizzled olive oil over and sprinkled salt and pepper before slipping it inside the oven.

While he was looking for all the salad ingredients his cell phone started to ring. He opened it without looking at the display of who was calling.

"Hello," he said, grabbing lettuce and tomatoes out of the fridge.

"It's Zero. Tiny's in a meeting at the moment, and he wanted me to give you an update."

Glancing toward the doorway, Lash made sure it was clear before continuing with the call.

"I'm free. Go on."

He closed the fridge, leaned over the counter and listened to what Zero had to say.

"Contact just confirmed David Marston is working for the Lions. He's gaining information to feed the rival group. Not only that, we've been given the heads-up on a new takeover assignment. Lions are planning on hitting us on our next ride."

Lash listened and cursed.

"Fuck, this is not going to go well. What's Tiny saying about it?"

"He's pissed. Hitting us on our turf and trying to take our town away, he's reaching out to the sheriff. He wants the town to know about what's going on," Zero said. "For them to be on alert in case something goes wrong."

"I hate those fucking pigs."

"You know what this means though, right?"

"Yeah, it means Angel's father has just become the most wanted guy to become dead." Lash shook his head, dropping it into his hands. "Between you and me, I was hoping this wasn't the case."

"We don't always get what we want, Lash. You know that otherwise your parents would be alive, and so would Tiny's woman. Shit happens."

Angel cleared her throat letting him know she was there. She stood naked but covered herself by the wall. Her head peeked around the corner, and she smiled at him. The smile went to his heart and straight down to his groin. She looked so fucking charming and sexy. He was ready to lose it again.

"I've got to go. Is there anything else?" he asked, not moving from his spot.

"Yeah, Tiny wants to throw off the scent of us knowing about what's going to happen. There's a party this Friday. A proper party, bring your girl, and be ready for some serious horny shit."

Zero hung up.

"Is everything okay?" Angel asked.

"Come here."

He would never talk to Angel about club business. Her father was involved, and he intended to keep her out of the loop as much as possible. She padded toward him, and when she was close enough, he pulled her against his side.

"Friday there's going to be a party. A real party. I'm going to want you by my side. We've got a few days to get you ready for it."

"You're scaring me with the real party talk. I thought you guys had real parties."

Lash chuckled. "Baby, they were tame shit in comparison to what usually happens at those parties."

"I don't know if I want to know."

"You're with me. You'll stay by my side, and I'll be the one who claims you. No one else." He kissed the top of her head wondering when he should tell her about her father.

Chapter Six

"So I heard about the party this Friday. It's going to be awesome," Tate said over the phone.

Angel sat on the sofa inside Lash's house. Tomorrow was Friday, and she was getting more nervous with every passing day. Lash wouldn't let her stay at the club, and whenever they visited the place she stayed firmly by his side. When she went into town, she had to call in a Prospect to go with her. Lash would rather leave her at his home while he dealt with business. Her only consolation was the fact Tate knew his number. The other woman had been phoning her daily.

"I know about the party. How did you find out?" Angel asked.

"In my usual sneaky ways. I heard Dad talking to Steven about it. I've got that killer red dress to try out, and I intend to use it."

Rolling her eyes, Angel glanced at the clock. Lash would be arriving in twenty minutes. He always called her to let her know when she should expect him. She cooked dinner and spent extra time cleaning his home. Angel liked to keep busy, and staying in his home when she wasn't earning a wage didn't sit well with her. Until her father settled his debts she was still part of down-payment to the club.

With how quickly Lash had taken her away from the club he could just as easily take her back.

She didn't want to get accustomed to a lifestyle she may not be able to keep up with.

"They'll flip when you turn up. You're the little biker princess, Tate."

"I'm a woman, and I intend to be treated like one."

Angel moved from the sofa into the kitchen to see how the stew was coming along.

"Don't you think you're acting a little drastic? I mean, it could blow up in your face if you're not careful."

Tate let out a sigh. "Can I be real honest with you?"

"Of course, we're friends."

"I fell really hard for Murphy when he was a Skull. I mean, I had this sick as fuck crush on him, and I'd do anything to gain his attention. It wasn't about who he was or what he could do. He was the first guy to show any interest in me. Everyone's terrified of my Dad, and that just plain sucks." Angel heard the sadness over the phone. "Then I found out he was a disloyal bastard and changed sides. He's been part of the Lions for a few years. Seeing him brings back all the shit I felt for him."

Angel listened as Tate bawled her eyes out over the phone. "I feel like a pathetic person. Do you think I'm pathetic?"

"No," Angel said, meaning it. "You allowed yourself to reach out to someone else, and they didn't want you. I don't think you're pathetic. If anything, I imagine you'll be more cautious."

"Murphy didn't even say goodbye. I mean, what could I have meant to him if I didn't even register in his shit little mind?"

Angel had noticed her friend got more vocal in her curse words when she was hurt.

"He's a complete dick for not treating you right, Tate."

Tate chuckled. "Hearing you say dick is kind of strange."

Rolling her eyes, Angel pulled the lid off the casserole and gave it a stir.

"From what I've been told I need to prepare myself for tomorrow. I don't think I'll ever be prepared."

"Have you ever seen a porn film?" Tate asked.

"No."

"Seriously? You've never seen people fucking or anything?"

"I've seen a couple of the members going at it but nothing explicit."

Silence fell over the line. "Wow, okay this is going to be a real eye-opener for you. The club has its own set of rules. Whatever goes down there sort of stays down there."

"Okay, please just tell me what's going on so I stop worrying. The way you and Lash talk I'm starting to think sacrifices, mass murder, and all kinds of things go on at these functions."

"Fucking, sharing, all kinds of nasty sex goes down. The members share the sweet-butts, and they don't always do it behind closed doors. All kinds of sex you can think of, anal, oral, and normal. Use your imagination, and it's happening."

"Wait, if you've never been to one then how do you know what happens?" Angel asked. Her hands were shaking, partly in fear and partly in excitement. What had happened to her? Lash had awakened something inside her, and now she couldn't shut it down. She felt controlled by it and not in a great way.

"Murphy told me. He was part of the party scenes. I complained about not going, and he told me straight everything that happened. He even showed me a video he'd taken on his cell phone of a woman being fucked in the ass, pussy, and mouth."

"I'm not ready for this," Angel said. "Lash and I haven't even done anything. I've never done anything with anyone else. I don't know what to do."

Panic clawed at her. She was so scared of everything that might happen she didn't even hear him come home. Lash took the phone out of her hand and placed it against his ear.

"I'm telling your father about this, Tate. My woman is petrified, and you're the one to blame." He listened for a few seconds and then shook his head. "No, I'll handle Angel." He pressed a button on the phone then placed it on the counter. "Tate shouldn't have been telling you anything of what's going on."

"You're taking me there tomorrow night. Don't you think I have a right to be prepared?" she asked. He moved her away from the stove and picked her up onto the counter. Even with her sat on the kitchen counter he was taller than her. It wasn't fair. He could distract her so easily and take away the concerns even though she was petrified of what might or might not happen.

"I can't tell you everything that happens because every party I've been to has been different. Yes, a girl was fucked by three men at the same time at one party, but the same woman didn't make an appearance at the next one. Everything is different. The men are different, and they change their minds to what they like or don't like." He started unbuttoning her shirt until he tugged it from her body.

Lash flicked the clasp of her bra open, and her breasts hung free. He cupped them in his hands before leaning down to take one nipple into his mouth. She cried out from the instant pleasure as he sucked on one of the buds. He moved to the other bud lavishing attention to both her nipples. Heat pooled between her thighs from his gentle suction on her breasts. When he touched her pussy, Angel knew she'd be dripping wet. There was no stopping her reaction to him.

He'd made her feel so much in a short time that she couldn't even think straight. She'd never had sex, yet she was sharing Lash's bed. He wouldn't let her sleep anywhere else but by his side, naked. Lash also hated clothes. No matter what she wore the minute they were alone he got her naked. She wasn't allowed to wear clothes in his presence, or at least that's the way he'd left her feeling.

His hands fell to her skirt, and in quick time that followed her shirt and bra along with the small panties she wore. "I don't know why you bother with underwear."

"I'm not used to not wearing any," she said.

"Well you better start getting used to not wearing any. I'm going to rip the shit out of them, and then you'll have no choice but to go bare." His palm settled on her pussy. "When are you going to get this baby waxed?" he asked.

"Tate has booked us both an appointment for tomorrow morning. She knows a place in town that's good." She hated the conversation she'd had with Tate over getting her waxed. It was completely embarrassing and humiliating, but she'd done what he asked, and tomorrow she was getting her pubic hair removed.

"Good, I'll have Prospect Steven accompany both of you," Lash said, going down to his knees in front of her.

She shook her head. "No, no way am I getting waxed with one of your men watching."

"Steven wouldn't be watching. He'd be sat outside in the waiting room like a good little Prospect."

Angel stared at Lash thinking about the jobs poor Steven had been handed because of her. "Why does he do it? Why does he put up with all the crap you and the crew give him?"

"He does it to earn his spot within the club. We all earn our place by doing all the shitty jobs. I'm not asking Steven to do something I haven't done before." He opened her thighs.

"Why? What's so important about the club? What makes The Skulls so special that men like Steven would put up with the shit you and others throw at him?" She placed a hand over his to stop him from advancing up her thigh.

"We're a family. We're not your run-of-the-mill-family, and we'll never be the type of guys who has the white picket fence and the lovely kids you see on the advertisement. We're not judgemental about our group. Anyone can join, and we don't take crap from outsiders. We're a family, Angel. We come from a lot of different families, but in the end it's only us stood side by side through thick and thin. That's why Steven will work his ass off, so he can earn his spot in this club. It's hard work, but it's worth every second of it." His hand pushed hers away. "Now are you going to let me eat this pussy or not?"

      ****

Tate was so going to get her ass kicked. Lash was going to make sure she got more than a stern talking to by Tiny. The only thing stopping him from phoning Tiny right now was the fact Angel was naked and in front of him. The scent of her pussy was driving him insane. He'd been waiting all day for another chance to taste her. Once was never enough and would never be enough for him.

"I'm sorry. I didn't mean to insult you," she said, biting her lip.

"You didn't insult me, baby. No one gets the club. I accept that, and I don't give a shit. Steven's a great guy and is showing real potential. The others, not so much."

"Who gets to decide who stays and who goes?" she asked.

"We vote. Now, I want to eat your pussy before I sit through dinner. Shut the fuck up so I can enjoy it."

Angel stared down at him, but Lash was determined to eat her sweet little pussy. He couldn't wait for her pubic hair to be removed so he could relish every part of her, but until then he was making do.

Opening the lips of her sex, he spotted her swollen pink slit. Licking his lips, Lash stuck out his tongue and started to caress the sweet nub. He loved going down on Angel. What he loved the most was the fact she wasn't tainted by any other man. He knew it was wrong to think like that about his woman seeing as he'd been with so many women. Lash couldn't deny the satisfaction of being the only one.

Her moans started to fill the air, and her knuckles were white where they gripped the edge of the counter. He wanted to fuck her so badly, but at the same time he was holding back, waiting for the right moment.

She deserved her first time to be perfect.

"Oh God, that feels so good." She cried out, her hands sinking into his hair as he sucked her clit into his mouth. Each time he took her the sweet little Angel he'd come to know let go some more. He couldn't imagine the straitlaced girl in the bar sinking her fingers into his hair.

Little by little she was blossoming into a beautiful, seductive woman. Lash wanted her to let go. He needed for her to let go of all of her inhibitions in order for her to become his old lady. That was never going to happen if she remained the same. Angel would need to be strong in order to stay by his side. Lash would spend every waking hour of the day to guarantee that.

"Oh God," she said again.

Feeling how close she was to exploding, Lash centred his attention on her clit, flicking the nub with his tongue. In a matter of moments Angel splintered apart in his arms. He slurped up her cum and brought her down gently from her orgasm.

She sat slumped on his kitchen counter. Her breasts quivered with each indrawn breath she took.

"I think this is the best my counter has ever looked," he said, wiping her juices from his chin and standing up.

A blush filled her cheeks, and her gaze looked past his shoulder. Reaching out, he wrapped his hand in her hair and brought her lips to his. He slammed his lips against hers taking control of her through his kiss alone.

Angel went from being tense to putty in his hands. She relaxed against him giving into what he wanted.

"They'll be more playtime later. Serve me dinner, woman," he said.

"I hate it when you get all male on me."

He helped her off the counter then slapped her ass on the way past. "Get used to it. I'm the one in control, and that's never going to change, not even for you."

She rubbed her bottom but didn't speak back to him again.

His hand had left a red print on her ass, and Lash shook his head.

Tearing his clothes off his body he headed toward the laundry room, picking Angel's clothes up on his way past. He stuffed them into the machine and filled it with powder before heading back to his woman.

Angel was serving them up some casserole as he took his seat at the table. He loved watching her work his kitchen. Her ass shook with every step she took. Lash loved the little jiggle of her ass and tits.

"Did you have a good day at work?" she asked, walking toward him. She carried both of their plates and put one in front of him.

"It was okay."

He didn't talk about club business with her. She was an old lady and a civilian. Tiny had taught him at a young age to keep club business to himself. When he'd asked why, Tiny had looked at Patricia, who'd still been alive, and told him rival clubs couldn't use their women against them.

It was known that The Skulls didn't tell their women their secrets. The women were left alone, and the men could function in peace without freaking out every time their women left the house. While the shit was going down with the Lions, Lash wanted his woman safe. He didn't trust any of the men from the rival group, and until Angel's father was taken care of, he was going to veer on the side of caution when it came to her.

Angel didn't push him for answers, and they ate their meal in silence. Once food was finished Lash took her up to their bathroom where he ran a bubble bath. They bathed together before he dried her body and led her back through to the main bedroom.

He was wiping the water from his body while she brushed her hair. Lash noticed her gaze was on him all the time she looked in the mirror.

"What's the matter, baby?" he asked.

"I was just wondering about your tattoos. I noticed all the guys have them." She pointed at his arm and chest.

Lash loved getting ink. The biggest tattoo he held was of the Fort Wills emblem of The Skulls. "They're a rite of passage and just some cool pictures. The tree was my idea, and I get an artist in the city to do mine. I'd never trust one of the guys to touch my skin."

"I noticed the tree had lines in the centre."

He gazed down his body to see what she was looking at. "Yep, I asked for them."

"Why?"

"I'm going to have the name of my woman and my kids in that tree. Tiny has a tattoo down his arm. He has the names of his woman and daughter. I think he even put Nash and my names on it seeing as he helped to raise us. I thought it was cool and decided that was what I was going to do."

She finished brushing her hair and moved past him to the bed. Her body was bare of any clothing. He'd banned clothing from bed. If she stepped foot inside his bed with clothing on, then he was spanking her ass.

"I like your ink," she said, staring at him. The bed covers were up to her chin as she stared at him. Shaking his head, Lash walked toward the bed. He gripped the edge of the blanket and tore it from her grip.

"I love your body, baby." He started at her foot, caressing her skin with the tips of his fingers. He travelled up, skimming over her sex and up further to her breasts. "Roll over."

He climbed on the bed as she moved onto her stomach. The curves of her ass called to him, and he settled at the bottom of the bed behind her.

Running both hands up her thighs he settled his palms on each ass check. She turned her head to look at him.

"Is Lash your real name?" she asked.

"No." He opened the cheeks of her ass to look at the puckered hole of her anus. Biting back a groan he slipped a hand underneath her to feel her soaking wet pussy. It would be so easy for him to slip inside her tight cunt, but he wouldn't do that. He wasn't ready for that.

Lash wanted her to see everything before he took that part of her.

Part of him wanted to claim her and make sure she couldn't walk away from him while another part needed her to accept him and the club for who they were.

She let out a moan, riding his palm as he teased her pussy.

"What's your real name?" she asked.

"You don't want to know." His father hadn't been allowed to name him. The name he'd been given came from his mother who'd been in a real pissed-off mood at the time.

"I do. You know my name, and I don't have a clue what your name is."

Letting out a sigh, he brought his wet fingers to her anus and started stroking that forbidden hole. Angel tensed, but he stroked the line of her back, stopping her from tensing around him.

"Nigel Myers, that's my name." He gritted his teeth as Angel turned her head to face him.

"Seriously?" Lash saw the humour in her eyes.

Shaking his head, he started laughing. "Dad didn't want to call me that. He pissed Mom off, and she wouldn't back down. She accepted the club and the shit, but she got to name his children. I don't even want to think what she'd name a girl." He shook his head remembering the horror on his Dad's face whenever he was called Nigel. Tiny and his Dad gave him a nickname, which, fortunately, stuck. "Mom named Nash, Edward. He hates the name and doesn't let anyone know it."

"I can't believe your name is Nigel. It's so … tame." She started laughing, and Lash couldn't help but do the same.

He stopped her laughter by pressing one finger into her ass. Her ring of muscles kept him out, but he pressed inside until she took him to the knuckle. Lash wasn't going to do anything more. Soon he'd take her ass and her cunt, but for now he was content to touch her like this.

"Well, it's nice to meet you, Nigel."

"Likewise, Angel."

Chapter Seven

Angel sat beside Lash as he took her into town. She was meeting Tate at the salon, and Steven was going to meet them there. Lash was determined to get her to her appointment. He held her hand all the way there. This morning they'd only spoken briefly, and nothing had come out about the party. When she was alone she felt nervous, but once Lash was beside her, she didn't feel anything other than the sensations he created when she was with him.

Several of the town folk stared in their direction, and when he pulled up outside of the salon they gained many more stares. He climbed out of the car then moved around to her side. Lash helped her out, grabbed something from the backseat, then shut the door.

"I thought you weren't going to make it," Tate said, walking toward them. She carried a black bag over her shoulder, and she was wearing tight jeans with The Skulls shirt.

Steven pulled up seconds later on a motorbike.

"I want you to wear this." Lash handed her a leather jacket.

"What is it?" she asked, opening it up to see a smaller symbol of The Skulls emblem on the jacket.

"It's our jacket. Our women wear them if they want to if they don't have a ring on their finger. I want you to wear it for me today." He stroked her cheek, pushing some of her hair off her face.

"Dude, we're getting waxed. She's going to be butt-ass naked for most of the day. She doesn't need your jacket," Tate said, rolling her eyes. There was a smile on her face, and Angel took that as a good sign.

"I don't mind. I'll wear it."

She handed Tate her bag and then eased the jacket over the small dress she was wearing.

Lash helped pull her hair out of the inside and settle it over.

"How does it look?" she asked.

His scent clung to the leather, and Angel knew she wasn't going to wear anything else. She didn't know how it had happened, but she was falling for him, in a big way.

"Sexy, baby." He dropped a kiss to her lips. "I'll pick you up later. We're going to the party together." Lash turned to Steven. "Keep me posted, and don't leave their side."

He climbed back into his car. She turned toward the salon when Lash whistled to gain her attention.

"Whatever you do, do not cut your hair," he said.

She pulled the length over one shoulder and nodded.

"Have fun."

Angel stayed long enough to watch the car disappear into the distance.

"Damn, he's got it bad for you, honey. I mean, really bad." Tate handed her back her purse, and together with Steven in tow they made their way into the salon.

Angel was nervous, and she hated the fact she was nervous. Steven kept a good distance as Tate signed them in. They were taken back to a changing area where they were asked to strip and to put their clothes in a locker.

"What do you mean?" Angel asked, when they were alone long enough to talk. Steven was outside in the waiting area, and the changing room was clear.

"I've known Lash a long time. He's practically my brother in a non-related kind of way. I've seen him with plenty of women. He's never been this possessive or protective with any of his other women. You're special.

You're different. I think it's cool," Tate said. "He cares about you, and he'd not just after sex either, which is good."

Angel looked at the other woman. "I didn't think anything of the way he was treating me. I thought he treated all the women the same."

"You're so wrong. A lot of the other girls hate him. He fucks and leaves them. Lash is not known for being with the same girl twice. It's what makes you special, and the bitches hate you more."

"How come none of the men or women talk back to you or anything?" Angel asked.

Tate wrapped a towel around her body and then a robe. "Seriously, you don't know?"

"I've not really made it my business to know about The Skulls lifestyle. I never thought I'd get anywhere close to them, let alone being potentially dating one," Angel said, hoping she explained it right.

"Honey, you're not dating. The Skulls don't date. You're Lash's woman. That's not dating. This is a big deal. Anyway, I get away with shit because I'm Tiny's daughter. The men were there when I was born or have known me a long time, and the women put up with me because Dad is the President of the club. They've got no choice. They start with me, and I can kick their ass to the curb."

Tate handed her another robe to put on.

Running a hand down the leather jacket, Angel didn't want to part with it. The leather still possessed Lash's scent.

"And from the look in your eye you've got it bad for Lash."

Angel smiled. "He told me his real name last night."

"No shit. Oh my God, that is a big deal."

77

Angel removed the jacket and placed a robe over her shoulder all the time Tate was talking.

"He hates the name Nigel. He thought his Mom was seriously unfair in naming it him."

"He told me Nash's, too."

"This is serious, Angel."

She smiled and nodded her head, but all the time she couldn't help but doubt it. Her father was still trying to gain back the money he'd lost, and until he'd done that, she was The Skulls' property.

They walked together as they got massaged and pampered. Angel loved her company and couldn't believe they'd never been friends before now. Tate was a little older than she was, and they did come from two different backgrounds.

"I heard about how your mother died. I'm really sorry you lost your Mom. It sucks," Tate said, pulling Angel out of her thoughts.

Tears filled her eyes as she thought about her mother. "She was really sick. I hate to say it, but I'm pleased she passed when she did. She was always in so much pain and tried not to show it. Mom was strong. She would have kicked Dad's ass if she knew what he'd gotten himself into."

"My Dad has never been the same since Mom died. He hired a nanny, and she stays around but he's never taken another woman. I imagine he fucks women at the club, but he doesn't bring anyone home."

Angel winced at her language.

"You do that a lot, you know?" Tate said.

"Huh? What?"

"When I say certain words you wince, and your face gets all scrunched up." Tate flicked her hand in the air. "If you're going to be Lash's woman you've got to learn to talk the talk and handle all the shit in between. It's the only way it'll happen."

They grew silent as their masseuses entered the room. Two well-built men with large muscles came toward them. Angel's heart-rate picked up.

"Do you think Lash and Tiny have any idea?" Angel asked.

"Nope, and I'm going to enjoy this while I can."

During the whole of the massage Angel couldn't get comfortable. She remained tense every time the guy touched her.

"Anyway, what was I saying, to be part of the club you need to stick up for yourself. Lash is not going to be by your side forever, and the bitches will descend. The old ladies will look out for you, though. We're all in a tight knit group, but they'll not be around all the time."

Angel opened her eyes to see Tate staring at her.

"I can't get comfortable." Angel mouthed the words at Tate and did her best not to look at the guy trying to massage her.

"I've got it covered." Tate leaned forward and started typing buttons into her cell.

"What are you doing?" Angel asked.

"Seeing how far Lash's protective streak goes." The cell phone was placed on the floor.

Angel remained tense while the man tried to work her muscles.

"You need to relax, and let me help you. You're too tense," the man said.

****

"Fuck, you've got to be kidding me," Lash said. The rest of the club looked at him as he slammed his cell phone down on the table.

"Do we even want to know what has got your panties in a twist?" Nash asked. He had Kate sat in his lap, and Lash watched the two with disgust. Kate had been with most of the crew, and still his brother was tapping it.

Tiny looked up from the paperwork he was working through. "Is there a problem?"

"Yeah, there's a fucking problem. Since when did the salon hire big, sexy men?" Lash asked, growling each word out.

"Do you need to tell us something, brother? Have you gone to the other side without telling us?" Nash joked making some of the men laugh.

Rolling his eyes he showed Nash the picture message Tate had sent him. He whistled, and in no time at all the cell phone got to Tiny.

"Those bastards are touching my daughter. Lash, save your woman, and get Steven to take over. I'd rather have a guy I know I can control massaging my daughter than those bastards."

Nash was laughing at him.

"Go and run after your chick," Nash said.

Going to his brother, Lash pulled him up by his arm.

"Hey, what are you doing?"

"If Steven's taking over from the big guy, then you're taking over from Steven."

Lash got the last laugh, and together they left the club. Kate's whining followed them out. He ignored her, straddled his bike, and broke every single speed limit getting to his woman.

Once outside the salon he walked in, grabbed Steven around the arm then headed in the direction of his woman.

"What's the matter, Lash? I've done everything you asked."

"Yeah, I know. When you have a woman of your own you'll understand."

Lash opened three doors and came up with nothing. On the last door he came to his woman. Her back was exposed and the towel lay across her bottom. If he hadn't seen how tense she was he would have seen red.

"Get your hands off my woman, and get the fuck out," Lash said.

"Lash!" Tate sounded pissed off.

"Lash," Angel said. His woman sounded relieved.

"We were only trying to give them a massage," the guy touching Tate said.

"I don't give a fuck. Get out now." He showed them the patch on his jacket, and the two men left the room.

Steven had a hand over his eyes as Tate sat up and covered her breasts with one arm while the towel hid her privates.

Lash wasn't affected by her. Tate was like a sister to him. However, Angel's naked body was something else. He'd gotten instantly hard at the sight of her.

"I knew you'd charge in here the moment you saw her. I knew it," Tate said, giggling.

"Yeah, your Dad knows, and Steven now has to be the one to give you a massage," Lash said, removing his jacket. He wore a plain black tee underneath. Moving toward his woman he saw her gaze on him as he got closer.

"What?" Tate asked, looking at the Prospect.

Steven's hand left his face as he looked horrified. "No, please, let me go out and watch. I don't want that job."

"You've already got one afraid of you, Tate."

Tate sent Steven a withering stare. "You better be good. I don't want my trip spoiled because of greasy, disgusting hands. You better wash your hands after you've used the bathroom."

"I did, and I do." Steven glanced over at him, pleading with his eyes. "I can do anything else but not this, please."

"Just get it over with," Tate said, settling back on her stomach.

Lash grabbed the oil from the stand by Angel's bed. He squirted some of the liquid onto her back before placing it on the stand. Rubbing his hands together to warm them up he coated his palms and started stroking across her skin.

Angel instantly relaxed against his touch. "That feels nice."

"It's a good job you didn't look comfortable with his hands on your body. I'd have killed him and spanked your ass," Lash said.

Tate snorted.

"I didn't want him touching me. I thought it was going to be a woman. I hoped it was a woman."

He dropped a kiss to her shoulder and started rubbing the oil into her flesh. Steven was doing the same. Lash saw the look of concentration on his face.

Seconds later the door opened, and Nash was leaning against the doorframe. He was eating an apple as he looked between the two women. Nash looked grossed out at the sight of Tate, but interest shone in his gaze when they landed on Angel.

"I didn't have a clue she was hiding such a great body. I would have made a play before you got the chance," Nash said.

It was a gut reaction. Lash grabbed the bottle of oil and threw it at his brother. Nash caught it in his grip, laughing.

"Stop picking on your brother, Edward," Angel said.

Nash stopped laughing and looked between the two. "You told her our names?"

Lash nodded. Tate's laughter filled the room.

"This is so fucking awesome. I love this girl," Tate said.

Leaning down, Lash brushed his lips across her nape. "That was awesome."

His brother stormed out of the room leaving them all alone. He finished the massage, and when the woman came to the room to inform the women the waxes were ready, Lash stopped what he was doing. Angel tensed up and stared at her retreating back.

"I don't want to do this," she said.

"It's easier the second time. The first time is always the hardest to deal with," Tate said.

Lash pulled a face. "I don't need to know what you do to your bits, Tate. Keep it to yourself."

"Whatever, asshole." Tate grabbed Angel's hand leading her out of the room. Lash dried his hands and followed Steven out to the main foyer. Nash was sat in a chair looking bored. He took a seat opposite his brother so he could watch him. Steven sat several seats away giving them extra room. He liked the Prospect. Steven was proving to be the best of all three Prospects.

"I can't believe you told her our real names," Nash said.

"She's going to be my old lady, Nash. I had to tell her my name." Lash rested one foot on his knee. He stared at the door wondering how Angel was getting on. His mind was at ease knowing Tate would be with her.

"Yeah, what are you going to do when she finds out about her Dad and the shit he's into?"

"I'll deal with it. You knew this was happening. I'm not into the Kates of this world."

"The Kates of this world put out without baggage. You're young. Why are you saddling yourself with a woman?" Nash asked.

Closing his eyes, Lash counted to ten to calm down.

"You don't get it. Angel is the one woman for me."

Nash shook his head but didn't say anything more. An hour later Angel and Tate came out of the changing rooms dressed. Angel wore his jacket, and pride filled him at seeing his mark on her even if it was in jacket form.

Angel kept her face down as he approached. He heard Tate organising a new appointment.

"It's okay, Angel. You'll be fine," Tate said.

Lash frowned looking between the two women.

Tate shook her head. He waited for the appointment date, and they headed out to the bikes. Steven was waiting beside his truck.

"I'm just going to say bye to Tate, okay?" he asked Angel.

"Sure, take all the time you need." Her voice was hoarse, and he frowned some more.

Walking toward the truck he saw Tate getting ready to climb inside.

"Tate?" She stopped to look at him. "What's wrong with Angel?"

She looked past his shoulder. "The wax thing didn't go well."

"What do you mean?"

"They have sound-proofed walls, and I'm surprised you didn't hear Angel scream. She was in a lot of pain. She hated it, and she was crying and the woman was panicking. In the end they cleared away everything and made sure there's plenty of lotion. They've given Angel some ointment to help. Make sure she uses it. I'm going to book us in for weekly appointments, Lash, until she gets used to the wax."

Guilt swamped Lash as Tate's words sank in. "She was in a lot of pain."

"I've never heard a woman scream like that. She's not good with pain I guess."

Lash looked behind him to see Angel stood perfectly still. If she couldn't stand pain, how was he supposed to claim her virginity?

"I'll leave her to you. I'll talk to her in the morning." Tate gave him a hug and left. Nash was already on his way back to the club. Going toward his woman, he enfolded her in his arms. Tears were glistening in her eyes.

"It really hurt, Lash. I didn't think it would hurt so bad."

He held her tight against him. "I'm sorry, baby."

"I hope you like it."

"I know I will, baby, and I'll show you." Lash kissed the top of her head and then made to straddle his bike. "Come on, let's go home." He handed her a helmet and fired up his bike. "Climb on the back, and wrap your arms around me."

He moaned as her legs wrapped around him. Her hands settled around his stomach. Lash took a moment to gain control of his senses before he pulled away and started for home. He looked forward to seeing what the salon did to her pussy. He knew she would look far better than what he imagined.

The ride went without event, and when he pulled into his driveway, Lash was desperate to see her. He waited for her to climb off, and then he climbed off after her. When he'd removed their helmets, he grabbed her hand leading her to the front door.

"What are you doing?" she asked. He unlocked the door, slammed his way inside, and kicked the door behind him.

"I asked you to get it done, and now I'm going to look at what I wanted." He didn't want to go upstairs to their room.

He went to the sitting room, kicked the wooden coffee table out of the way, and tugged her to his side.

Lash pushed her chestnut hair off her face and then slammed his lips down on hers. Plunging his tongue into her mouth, Lash let out a moan, consuming her with his lips. She relented to him, giving him her mouth for a kiss. He wasn't just falling for her. Lash had fallen for her and fallen hard.

Breaking from the kiss he rested his head against hers. "Wow," she said. "It was totally worth it just from the kiss."

He chuckled. Fingering the button of her jeans Lash opened her button and slid her jeans down to the floor. She must have taken a spare pair of clothing with her. The small dress she wore wouldn't have been good to wear on the back of his bike.

They didn't have time to do anything more. The party would be starting soon, and Lash wanted to take Angel before the real shit happened. He pressed her down to the sofa and settled between her thighs. Gripping her knees he tugged her to the edge of the sofa, opening her thighs wide.

All the time he kept his gaze on hers. Green eyes glistened back at him waiting.

"Why aren't you looking?" she asked, nibbling her lip.

"I'll look at my pussy in all good time." He kept his gaze on hers before sliding his attention down to rest on her pretty *bare* pussy. She looked a little sore, but the ointment the woman gave her had stopped it from hurting. In a few hours she'd be completely fine.

Running his fingers over the lips of her pussy Lash smiled. "You look so fucking beautiful. I'll give you a few days to keep with the ointment, but then I'm eating you up."

He saw her pussy cream at his spoken words. His woman wanted to be fucked, licked, and made love to just as much as he wanted to.

Caressing up and down her thighs Lash grew frustrated. All he wanted to do was fuck his woman, but he had a party to attend. "Come on, we need to get you ready for the party." He dropped a kiss to her hip and then stood.

Chapter Eight

"Stop fucking fidgeting," Lash said, growling the words. Angel glared at him. It was all right for him. He was wearing leather pants, a tee, and a jacket. What did she have to wear? A small skirt that came to mid-thigh, a crop top that only just covered her stomach. At his request she only wore a bra and a pair of six inch stiletto heels. She couldn't walk in the heels, and she was taking some practice walks down his long hall way. Her hands were outstretched for balance, and Lash was watching her.

She glanced over at him to see him smiling, which made his words less aggressive. Angel needed to get used to the way he talked. In her home when someone swore it was because they were annoyed.

"Stop laughing at me. I told you I can't walk in these." She squealed, but Lash reached out to catch her as she started to fall.

"Okay, I've got you, and the bitches can be hard at times. Right, we'll go for smaller heels until you can work up to the tall heel."

He picked out a pair of two inch heels. "Here, put these on?" Lash handed her another pair of shoes.

She used him as a stand to remove her shoes. Lash helped her to put the new pair of shoes on. He finished off her outfit with his leather jacket. "This is so everyone will know you're my woman."

Angel didn't mind wearing the jacket. She loved his smell and smiled as it surrounded her.

"I love your smile." He stroked her cheek. His compliment touched her. "I love the skirt, baby, but I've got to be responsible." Lash pulled out a pair of jeans from the drawer. "Put these on."

Angel took them out of his hands and climbed into them. They were loose enough for her to do. When she was finished, Lash nodded. "It's too fucking dangerous riding on a bike in a skirt. Take them off as soon as we get there, okay?"

She nodded in agreement.

"Come on, let's get out of here before something happens at the party."

He took her hand leading her out to his bike.

"We're not going in your car?" she asked, approaching his bike.

"Not tonight. It's all about the bike."

She tugged on the skirt trying to pull it down and then remembered the jeans she wore. Angel shook her head, laughing.

"If you keep pulling it down it's going to end up around your knees. The jeans cover everything," he said, warning her.

Letting go of the skirt and rubbing her hands down the jeans, she waited for Lash to pass her a helmet. He straddled a bike then waited for her to climb on behind it. The jeans weren't tight, and she was able to straddle him without fear.

She loved riding on his bike. There was something freeing about letting everything out and speeding on the open road. She wished she could feel it without the helmet on, but for now she was happy to be safe on the back of his bike.

Holding onto his waist, she rested her chin on his shoulder. With her arms wrapped around his waist Angel didn't feel any nervousness about the upcoming party. Whenever she was with Lash all of her nerves left her as if they had no right being there.

Closing her eyes she let the peace she felt swamp her. Lash may be the total opposite of what she wanted out of a man, but she wasn't going to turn him away because of her old plans.

She really was falling for Lash, or Nigel Myers, and she really believed she may even be in love with him. Letting out a sigh, Angel kept her eyes closed relishing the feel of being close to him.

"Are you okay?" he asked.

"I'm fine."

One of his hands covered hers where they were wrapped around his waist. "I've got you, baby."

Angel really hoped that was true because with each minute she felt she was losing her heart to this man.

He pulled into the forecourt of the bar, which was already crowded with bikers, women, and men. That was how she divided the groups. There were bikers, and then there were men. Lash was a biker while her father was just a man.

What the hell was going on inside her head? There was a time when all men were grouped together.

Lash turned off his bike, and several bikers and women surrounded him. He removed his helmet and shook hands with a guy she recognised as Zero.

"It's great to have you back."

She handed her helmet to Lash then started climbing off, shocked when a pair of hands helped her off the bike. Glancing over her shoulder she saw Nash stood helping her.

"Thank you," she said.

"You're Lash's girl. I'm all for helping out his girl." Nash smiled at her before wrapping his arms back around Kate. The other woman glared at her jacket.

"She's really been claimed by Lash?" Kate asked, pouting.

"Shut the fuck up." Nash growled the words, and then they were moving away.

Lash's arms banded around her waist and pulled her close to his body. His fingers opened the jeans, and they were sliding down to the floor. "My brother is being nice. He might actually like you." He kissed her neck. "Pass me the jeans." She bent down, retrieving the jeans from the floor.

"Or he's trying to scare me away." Lash put the jeans across his bike.

"Nash wouldn't go to that much effort."

She smiled and turned in his arms.

"Besides, I think he's going easy on you because of the party. Things will get interesting real soon. Come on, let's go and mingle."

He took her hand leading her away from the bike and into the crowd of people. Bikers and men stopped him in their path. A few of the women tried to gain his attention, but he'd pull her against him and once they saw her they scampered away.

"Tiny's inside, man. He looks ready to do murder," Butch said.

"Okay, I'll go and see him."

Lash took her through to the main bar. A couple of women were giving a strip tease on top of the tables. Angel noticed one of the women was an old lady, and her man was watching her intently.

"That's Hardy and Rose. They're a strange couple, and he loves watching men salivate over what's his. None of the guys are allowed to touch her. They can watch but not touch."

"She's beautiful," Angel said, staring at her red hair and pale complexion.

"She is, and she's a lovely woman devoted to Hardy. They're a team, and he does everything to protect and love her. Depending on his mood he'll fuck his woman in front of them, but again, they watch and don't touch. He likes to torture the men."

They stood watching the show. Angel saw how Rose's gaze was on Hardy the whole time. The men were enthralled by her dancing. She felt an answering heat in her groin but didn't say anything.

"Come on, Tiny's over there downing shots." Lash pulled her toward the bar.

"I hate women. I hate them all," Tiny said, downing another shot.

Lash took a seat pulling her onto his lap. Tiny sneered at her before taking another shot.

"Why are you hating women?" Lash asked, ordering two beers. He gave one to Angel. She took the beer wondering if she could pretend to drink it.

"They're a pain in the ass. Nanny wants me to let her go. She doesn't want to work for me anymore."

Angel didn't know much about Tiny's personal life, but she'd heard that he hired a nanny to take care of Tate. The woman he'd hired was eighteen at the time, but that was over ten years ago. Angel knew she must be either the same age as Lash or older. Tate was twenty-three, but Tiny still treated her like a baby, at least that was Tate's complaint to Angel.

"Eva's twenty-nine, Tiny. She wants to get out and spread her wings. You've had her in your employ for ten years. She's been loyal to you. Let her go," Lash said.

Tiny glared at Lash. The two men stared at each other, and Angel couldn't help but think they were communicating something.

"Okay, right. Then you need to do something about that, man. I can't help you." Lash downed his beer, slapped Tiny on the back then moved away, taking her with him.

"What was that all about?" she asked, following him.

"Men stuff, baby. Come on, let's get outside. I want to do some dancing."

She was pulled outside. Angel wondered how she was going to keep up when Lash suddenly stopped.

"You've got to be fucking kidding me."

Glancing over his shoulder she saw what he was looking at. A smile broke out over her face when she saw Tate gliding toward them wearing the killer red dress. The bikers stared at her shocked while the men drooled. Lash went tense.

"Where is he?" Tate asked, folding her arms. Her gaze went to Angel, and she smiled. "Hi, Angel." The anger returned as she glared at Lash. "Where's my fuck-head of a father?"

"You shouldn't be here." Lash folded his arms over his chest and glared.

"I don't give a fuck what you think, Nigel. Get out of my way."

No one ever called Lash by his real name. Silence met her answer.

"What is all the chaos about?" Tiny asked, coming up behind Angel. He looked at his daughter, and any buzz he was getting from the shots, clearly disappeared. "What the fuck are you doing here? And why are you dressed like that?"

"What did you do to Eva? She's locked herself in her room, and I can hear her crying. She won't let me near her." Tate's hands went to her hips. She glared at her father and looked ready to commit murder.

"She's not your concern." Tiny forced his way through. Lash's arms went around Angel as they watched father and daughter argue.

"Hello! She's my fucking nanny. Yeah, I get the joke, a grown woman with a nanny. Stop being a bastard and go to her." Tate looked hurt and angry.

Angel wondered who Eva was and what she meant to Tate's family.

"This is a party, Tate. You shouldn't be here and not dressed like that. Steven, take her home and make sure she stays there."

"If you so much as touch me I'll castrate you with my heels." The heels did look pretty dangerous. "If you send me home I'll make sure Eva comes back here to see you. Do you want her here?"

Tiny paled at Tate's words.

Lash cursed. "They're both as bad as each other. Neither of them can back away from a fight."

"You wouldn't fucking dare."

"Try me, Dad. I'm this close to losing it with you. I hate it when Eva cries, and so do you." Tate flipped out her cell phone. "One call will get her here."

They stared at each other, and even Angel tensed waiting for her answer.

"Steven, she stays, and if anyone hurts her it's your ass I'm taking it out of." Tiny stormed away. "I need a fucking drink and a woman."

Angel noticed none of the women went to him.
****

Lash watched his leader and mentor storm around to the back of the building. Angel stayed by his side, but he needed to go and make sure Tiny was okay. Tate moved closer to them.

"I hate it when he gets like this," Tate said, hand on hip. She was gaining attention from some of the men. Tate glared in their direction. Lash never felt the need to protect her as she always knew how to take care of herself. "What the fuck are you looking at?"

95

She shook her head in disgust then grabbed Angel's arm. "I know you're going to want to talk to him. I'm taking her away from you for a while."

He kept a firm grip on his woman. Shooting a glare to Tate he waited until she left to go sit at the bar. Steven followed her.

"Okay, I guess you're about to leave me to go and deal with Tiny," Angel said.

"I've got to make sure he's doing good." He cupped her cheek and pulled her in close. "Until then, you'll stay at the bar. Steven will take care of you, and you'll have nothing to worry about." He fingered the jacket and knew in his heart she'd be safe. No one would try anything unless they wanted to start a war with all of The Skulls.

"Go be with Tate. I'll be back as soon as I can." He waited until she was sat next to Tate before heading off in the direction of Tiny.

He found him with Nash behind the back of the bar. The back faced a mass of forests and clear space. There were many times when he'd come here to think when he was growing up.

Tiny and his brother were smoking a cigarette.

"She shouldn't be here dressed like that. Why does she try to test me?" Tiny asked, staring up at the sky.

"Tate's hurting." Lash lit a smoke and stared out at the distance. He was surprised to see Nash without a woman on his arm.

"I yelled at Eva when she asked if she should be looking for another job. I told her to keep her ass where I told her to and if she wanted to do something useful she should start doing as she's told." Tiny sighed. "I was a fucking pig to her. I called her fat and useless. I hurt her."

Lash shook his head. Eva wasn't fat. She was rounded in all the right places but a little bigger than Angel. When he looked at Eva he was always reminded of a woman who'd be a loving mother. He'd seen her with kids and knew she was gentle at heart. Tiny saying stuff like that would hurt her feelings.

"Tate's a little old to be having a nanny. You've got to figure out what to do about Eva. She's got a life to live, too." Lash took a deep draw on his smoke and thought about Angel. He was taking her tonight. Staring at Hardy and Rose, he knew he wanted something similar to what they had. The commitment and the trust shone brightly between them.

"She's been part of my life since Patricia died. Eva cooks, cleans, and takes care of everything." Tiny shook his head laughing. "I can run this fucking town and keep my bikers happy, but the thought of running my home alone terrifies me. Patricia loved that house, and I want it to stay that way."

Lash knew there was more to Tiny's anger, and he was keeping it to himself.

Tiny finished off his cigarette.

"Tate doesn't know about Murphy, does she? That's why she's at the party and trying to give me a heart attack," Tiny said.

"She's hurting because he left. I think she was in love with him, and he betrayed her," Nash said, surprising Lash.

"I need to get a woman under me or seriously drunk. I'm going back inside. I suggest you two do the same. We've got a lot of work to do in the next week." Tiny left them alone.

"Where's Kate?" Lash asked.

"Probably giving some other guy a fuck. I don't know. Tiny needed someone, and you were dealing with

Angel. Shit is going to hit the fan soon. Do you realise this could be our last real party together?" Nash said, looking out at the scenery.

"Don't talk like that," Lash said. "We've been through worse."

"I don't know. It just don't feel right to me." Nash was silent for a few seconds. "Do you think Mom and Dad would approve of how we are?"

"I really don't know." Lash tried not to think of what his mother and father would think.

"We can't change it now. I suggest you get back to your woman. She looks hot."

Lash chuckled and hit out at his brother. "Keep your dirty hands off my woman."

They headed around the front of the club. In the short time they'd been away things had already started to spice up. Women were all in different states of undress. He passed one woman who was giving a biker a blow job and another guy a hand job. Shit, he needed to get inside the bar. Everything always got worse inside the club. Going to the door he paused when he saw Tate dancing on one of the tables. Steven was stood between two tables talking, and then he saw Angel on the other table. His woman was obstructed by Tate's form, but now he saw her clearly.

She was drinking from a bottle and dancing to the erotic pulse of the music playing in the background. Both women were beautiful and entirely out of place. Neither of them was dancing in order to gain attention, but from the panting looks of the men around them, they were rocking the moves. They were both smiling at each other, and Angel looked fresh-faced while Tate finally looked free.

"Lash, whoop, come here, buddy," Tate said, yelling over the music. "Angel's awesome."

His woman turned to him with a smile. She wasn't drunk, but she was a little merry. He saw that in the way she smiled at him. There was still a hint of reserve to her.

Walking toward her, Lash made his way through the crowd of people to get to Angel's table.

"Hi," she said. Her hips swung from side to side.

"Hi yourself."

"Are you angry with me?" She pouted at him, and he found the action incredibly cute.

"I leave you alone for two minutes, and you're dancing sexily on a table. What do you think?" he asked.

"You don't look angry. You've got your sexy smile on. I like your sexy smile. It does nice things down here." Her hand went between her thighs.

Lash hauled himself up on the table and grabbed her hand as whistles met her actions. Angel may not realise it, but she was winning their vote on her being his old lady. Wrapping his arm around her waist, he held her tight against him. "I'm the only one who can touch your pussy."

"I want you to touch me. I'm burning inside. Please, Lash." Her arms went around his neck. There was no way he'd take her in this current state. The rest of the night she was not drinking anything. He was going to have her sober.

Taking the bottle from her fingers, he took a long gulp of the burning whiskey. Glancing toward the bar he didn't see Mikey. Whoever gave his woman whiskey was going to feel his fist.

"Come on, you can dance for me." He helped her down to her feet, and several bikers cheered. Next, Lash grabbed Tate and handed her to Steven. "Keep her out of trouble. If Tiny finds out you'll be lucky to have a cock left."

He took Angel outside to help her sober up. Her arms were wrapped around his neck, holding onto him.

"I like this party, Lash. It's fun."

Leaning against a wall he tugged her between his legs. She wiggled her body next to his making him moan.

"I think that's the whiskey talking."

Her hand landed on his cock, rubbing him through his jeans. "Fuck, baby."

"I know what I'm talking about, and I want to do to you what you do to me, Lash. I'm not drunk. I know what I'm doing."

Before he could say anything she sank to her knees in front of him.

"Angel, what are you doing?"

"I'm giving you pleasure. I've seen a couple of the girls do it, and now I want to do it to you." She fumbled with the tie in his leather pants.

Lash stopped her. She looked up at him with such an endearing smile on her lips. "I can't let you do this."

"Why not? You've licked my pussy. I've even got all the hair ripped off to please you. I want to do this, please, Lash. I really do."

She tugged on his pants even as she stuck her lip out. Lash growled in annoyance and released his pants. He was going to regret this, but he couldn't stand to see the hurt on her face. She looked like he'd hurt her cat or something.

Angel pulled his pants down to his thighs, and his cock sprang out. He was so turned on by her dancing and everything about her, he was ready to explode. Her hands wrapped around his length, pumping the shaft with her tight, little fist.

"Fuck, baby, that feels good." He stared down at her, watching her ministrations on his cock.

She ran her finger through the slit of his cock, coating her fingers with his leaking pre-cum.

"What's this?"

"That's my cum," he said.

Angel pressed a finger to her lips, tasting him. In the next breath her mouth was on him.

Her inexperience drove Lash wild. In the weeks and months to come he hoped to teach her how to suck him properly, but for now he loved the way she took him into her mouth. There was a hesitancy about her. She took him until he hit the back of her throat and then stopped. He watched her head bob as she took him in her mouth. The rest of the club faded into the background. Lash savoured every second of Angel and her mouth on him.

His balls tightened, and with two quick thrusts inside her mouth he erupted filling her with his seed. Surprise gripped him as she swallowed him down. She didn't hesitate, merely swallowed him down, and he couldn't believe it. His little virgin looked so happy when she rested her head against his thigh.

"Did I give you pleasure?" she asked.

"You've got no idea how much pleasure you've given me."

Chapter Nine

Later that night Angel sat in the corner of the bar while Lash played cards with a couple of the club members. The party was starting to die down, but she'd gotten an eyeful throughout the night. After she'd given Lash a blow job, which she loved, the party came apart at the seams. They'd walked back into the bar in time to see Hardy penetrate Rose. Angel had been so shocked and turned on by what she'd seen that she'd stood and watched. Lash hadn't spoken a word throughout. He'd stood behind her with his arms wrapped around her waist, holding her against him.

The love was clear to see shining between Hardy and Rose. She wished things were different for her and Lash. Angel knew she was falling hard for him and may already be in love with him. She wanted to change for him and be what he needed in a woman. When Tate handed her the whiskey she'd felt the instant buzz, so that when her friend jumped up on the table, she'd followed suit.

After Rose and Hardy left to go to a private room, several of the sweet-butts had taken on the men. She never knew four men could fuck one woman before. Not only had she seen that, but she'd watched one of the men penetrate one woman before going to another and he'd switched between them throughout. She'd never be able to handle such crass attention. Lash didn't seem fazed by the happenings in the club. It was only when Tiny took a woman through to his office that Lash tensed up.

Nash had spoken up and told him to leave it alone.

Angel kept her nose out of it. Her first ever party had been a success in her mind.

"How are you doing over there, Angel?" Zero asked. He was playing cards with her man. Hardy and Rose had come back down, and Hardy was playing cards while Rose did a little light clearing up.

"I'm sober."

"Good, because we'll be leaving soon," Lash said, stroking her thigh.

She moaned, opening her thighs wider for him.

"I never thought I'd see the day when Angel Marston would stand on the tables and dance like that," Kate said, taking a seat on Nash's lap.

Nash slapped her ass warning her to be quiet.

"What? I'm only speaking the truth. I wonder who she was dancing for," Kate said, continuing to speak.

"I wasn't dancing for anyone. I joined my friend up on the table and had some fun. I wasn't doing anything wrong." Angel rested her head against Lash's arm. He smiled down at her as she smiled up at him.

"I think you're a natural, honey," Rose said, taking a seat beside Hardy. "Besides, we old ladies need to stick together. We're the ones that are going to stick around." Rose shot a glare at Kate.

"Put the claws away, kitten." Hardy kissed his woman.

Angel watched the interplay. She saw the respect the guys had for Rose and the lack of it toward Kate. The other woman really was anyone's piece of ass.

Lash slammed his cards on the table. "I'm out, fuckers. See you tomorrow." He got up from the table, slapped the guys' hands and together they made their way toward his bike.

"We didn't need to go if you didn't want to," Angel said. She'd been enjoying the banter.

"I only stayed longer for you to sober up." He cupped her ass, rubbing his crotch against the front of her body. "If I'd taken you home I wouldn't have controlled myself. Your first time, you're going to remember it."

From all the coffee he'd given her she was as sober as they came.

"Take me home, Lash." She snuggled close, inhaling his masculine scent. Lash handed her the jeans, which she put on.

He climbed on the bike, and she straddled the bike behind him. Lash handed her a helmet again, and she held on tighter than ever before. The drive back to his place was far more liberating than the drive to the club. She felt freer in mind and in spirit as they raced for home. She loved the feeling of the fresh air even in the darkness. Angel squealed and giggled. She felt Lash do the same.

When they pulled up into his driveway, she was turned on and ready for whatever Lash had to offer. The jeans and helmet were removed the instant she stepped off the bike.

Like all the other times before, he took control. Grabbing her hand he opened and locked his front door behind them. He didn't wait around to turn on lights but went straight upstairs to the bedroom.

Once inside Angel gasped as Lash sank a hand into her hair and his other hand curved around her waist. He brought her close, pressing his lips to hers. Closing her eyes, she opened her lips to receive his passionate kisses. His tongue traced her lips before plunging inside. There was no stopping his touch. The hand in her hair tightened to a fist pulling on strands of her hair. She gasped from the slight pain but didn't pull away from him.

His other hand moved from her hip to the jacket. He tore the jacket from her body and broke the kiss to finish his work. Lash pushed the hair off her face, staring into her eyes.

"So fucking beautiful," he said, possessing her mouth once again.

She didn't argue with him and kissed him back with the same passion he'd built up inside her. There was no mistaking the need he'd built up inside her over the past week alone. His touch set a fire, and she needed for him to finally put the fire out.

Running her hands up his thick arms, Angel moaned, loving the feel of his rippling muscles beneath her touch.

"I'm so hard for you." He trailed kisses down her jaw 'til he sucked in the flesh of her neck. Goose-bumps erupted all over her body from his touch. His hands held her steady while he sucked the hell out of her neck, marking her. There was no way she wouldn't be marked from his touch.

"I need you so bad." Lash pulled away once again. His fingers found the hem of her shirt, and he tugged it over her head. With quick movements he dispensed of her bra. His hands soon replaced her bra, cupping her in his palms. "Love your big tits. I have to taste."

Angel couldn't speak as Lash spoke and touched. He was the one in control, not her. His mouth was on her breasts, kissing, sucking, and biting down on her nipples. She watched him play with her like a musician did an instrument.

"So full and mine." Lash stepped back and tugged his shirt off. She grabbed the laces of his leather pants and helped him get rid of them from his body. They were both chuckling and rushing in their haste to get naked.

Within minutes they crashed to the bed totally naked and ready for each other. Lash knelt up, and Angel followed his movements, kneeling close to him. "We're finally here," he said, wrapping her hair around his arm.

"We are." Her voice sounded croaky even to her.

Lash reached out with his free hand and stroked her cheek. His cock pressed into her stomach. The thick brand of his cock was rock hard. Only hours ago she'd felt him explode inside her mouth. Licking her lips she gazed down at the hard shaft wondering what it would feel like to have that monster penetrating her pussy.

"I need you so bad."

"Take me, Lash. I'm here, and I'm all yours." She stared at his lips needing him to make the first move.

I'm going to have sex.

I'm going to have sex, and I'm terrified, excited, and I want him to take me already.

Lash leaned in and nipped at her lips, playfully. She followed his lead, smiling as he rubbed her nose with his. Angel ran her hands all over his tattooed body. His muscles were hard, tight, and totally hot. She didn't know how she'd gotten so lucky to have such a sexy man holding her.

With his free hand he stroked a path down her body setting a fire with his touch. Down her side, across her hip and between her thighs where he cupped her with his palm.

"Baby, you're so wet for me." She became aware of her bare pussy. He hadn't even touched her properly, and he felt her wetness.

He smiled at her. "The lips of your pussy are soaking, baby. This is why I wanted you bare. It's easy to feel your response. I love your cream." To prove his point he pressed his finger into his mouth, sucking her juices from the digit.

"Please, Lash, stop making me wait. I want you to be my first." *My only*. She added the last bit in her mind. Angel didn't want to voice the last part out in case he backed away. Lash had broken through her defences and her ideals, and now all she wanted was him. Her future, in her mind, contained only him.

****

Lash wanted to say so much more to her, but he held the words back afraid of how she'd react. He could take most things handed to him. Right now with her naked in his arms, Lash couldn't handle her rejection if it came. He never considered himself a coward and he never backed down from a fight, but for the first time in his life, he was backing down … at least for tonight.

He unwrapped his hand from her hair and settled her down on the bed. "Lie down, and open your thighs."

His Angel did as he instructed, lying against the pillows splaying her legs open wide. Kissing her lips one final time Lash moved down her body settling between her thighs. He wasn't going to lick her, but he was going to make sure she was nice and wet for him. Any excuse to look at her pussy and he'd take it.

"What are you doing? I thought you couldn't … you know … lick it?" Angel asked. He imagined her cringing after she spoke the words, and he chuckled.

"We're going to have to teach you the sex talk, baby." Not tonight. They could talk about the sex lingo another time.

He made himself comfortable and opened the lips of her sex. She was pale, smooth with a small blush from her wax. In time the blush would fade as she got used to being without pubic hair. Lash stroked his fingers over her pussy. Angel shuddered underneath him.

"It's sensitive," she said.

Lash smiled. Gazing down at her pussy, he worked the lips of her sex open for him to get a closer look. Her clit was swollen, and her cream was glistening. His virgin Angel was ready for him. Still, a bit more teasing wouldn't hurt. Pressing a finger to her clit, he gently stroked and teased until she was screaming his name.

Climbing up the bed he pressed the finger he'd touched her with to her mouth. "Taste yourself."

She opened her lips, sucking her cream from his finger.

"How do you taste?" he asked.

"Not as good as you," she said.

He growled, pressing his lips to hers. "Soon I'm going to feast on your pussy, but until then I'm going to make you mine."

Rearing back, Lash moved closer between her thighs, rubbing his cock through the slit of her pussy.

"Shouldn't you wear a condom?" she asked.

Lash frowned. "I'm clean, and I know you are."

"I've never been with a guy, so I'm not on the pill." She licked her lips, staring at him.

"So?" He waited for her to elaborate further.

"I could get pregnant," she said.

He smiled, rubbing his cock through her slit, coating him with her cream. Lash was larger than she was, but it felt right. He didn't feel like she was going to break on him.

"I don't care," he said, claiming her lips once again.

With his hand between their bodies, he guided his cock to her entrance. Slamming his tongue into her mouth, he distracted her enough to align his cock with her cunt and thrust deep inside her.

Angel's eyes opened wide, and she tried to push him away. Lash held her flailing arms over her head to stop her from hurting him or herself.

He broke the kiss, feeling her pussy ripple around him.

She whimpered, and tears filled her eyes. "You're hurting me. You're too big. Please, stop."

"I'm not too big. Just give it a second."

She shook her head, but there was no way Lash could leave her. He was bigger than she was, but the first time always hurt for a woman. Lash made sure he stayed perfectly still within her.

"You're hurting me. You promised not to hurt me."

"The first time hurts for every woman." He stared down in her face refusing to break contact. Her lips wobbled, and tears left the corner of her eyes.

"I want you to get off me."

Biting his lip, Lash swallowed past the lump in his throat. "Give it a couple of minutes, and if it still hurts I'll stop. This is supposed to happen."

Lash prayed to God she wasn't in pain, and if she was, he prayed again that he'd have the strength to stop.

"I'm going to let go of your hands, okay. You can touch me all you want. Just don't fight me, okay?"

"I won't fight you."

He released her hands and held himself off her body but so he was joined with his cock inside her.

She didn't fight him or reach out to touch him. He teased with the ends of her chestnut hair, waiting for her to speak.

Her hands lay where he'd left them. Leaning on one hand, he wiped the tears from her face. "You shouldn't be crying."

He hoped to God he hadn't fucked this up. The last thing he wanted to do was force her, but he felt like he was doing exactly that with making her wait and see if she was still in pain.

Slowly, the tears subsided, and Angel raised her hand to his face. She stroked his cheek, and he knew she was feeling the stubble on his face and chin. Her touch moved to the left side of his face, and her fingers were tracing his scar.

"How did you get this scar?" she asked.

"A fight with the Lions. He used a piece of glass on my face."

"Did you kick his ass?" She stared at the scar, and he saw the frown on her face.

"I beat the shit out of him, and he landed in jail for using the same piece of glass on an officer."

Her gaze met his. "I'm glad. I don't like the thought of anyone hurting you."

"Most of the time the bruises will fade, and you'll have nothing to worry about."

"I'm not worried about me, Lash. I'm worried about you. What happens if next time you're not able to get away? I would hate for you to be hurt." She dropped her hand to his chest. His heart beat rapidly against his chest.

"I'm a strong man and quick. The club is part of who I am, and I help protect it."

"Don't risk your life for it, Lash. Please," she said, begging him.

Angel didn't even know he'd risk his life for her.

"Baby, you know my cock is inside you right now, and you're wanting a serious conversation?" he asked, trying to make light.

"You've taken my virginity," she said, catching him off guard.

"Yes, I have." His cock pulsed realising he'd deflowered his woman. No other man was ever going to know the pleasure or feel of her tight cunt. Only him.

"You're happy about that," she said.

"Baby, you're all mine."

He leaned down, brushing his lips against hers. Her hand was trapped against his heart. She didn't have any idea how much she meant to him. Angel was the only woman who'd ever have a real place in his heart and his life. All the other women who'd come before her meant nothing.

"Lash?" she said, kissing him back.

"Yeah, sweetness."

"You can move now. It doesn't hurt anymore."

Pulling away he stared down in her eyes. "Are you sure?"

"Yeah, I want you to move." Her hands went to his forearms holding onto him.

Her pussy clenched around his cock like a fist. "I'll only move if you're sure."

"I want you, Lash. Please, finish what you started."

She arched up toward him. Her cunt tightened further, and he knew she was doing it.

Taking hold of her hands in his, he locked them by her head.

"I'm ready, Lash."

He took her at her word and eased out of her tight heat. She let out a moan but didn't fight him. Gazing down between them, he watched her cream glisten on his shaft. When only the tip remained inside he looked up into her eyes.

"Are you sure?"

She nodded and closed her eyes. The expression on her face showed wonder. Lash stared at her face watching the different emotions flit across her face as he slowly made love to her. He eased into her tight heat, swivelled his hips and pulled out. There was no rush to his movements. He drew everything out, loving the way she responded to his touch. Her hands tightened on his forearms, and Lash knew, without a doubt, that he was lost to everything else.

He felt each ripple of her pussy. She was close to coming. Angel thrust up to meet him, and together they made love. Lash felt he was making love for the first time. The emotions consuming him were unlike anything he'd ever felt before. Leaving one of her hands beside her head, he reached down and stroked her clit.

"I want you to come for me, baby," he said.

The touches on her clit made her cunt tighten around him. Groaning out at the pleasure, Lash stayed still waiting for Angel to come before he let himself explode over the edge.

This was a night of firsts. He was Angel's first and last man, and she was the first woman he'd ever cared enough about to make love to. She was his whole world, and he wasn't letting her go. No matter what she thought about him after the problem with her Dad was handled. He'd make her love him.

"Lash," she said, crying out.

Her cunt tightened, and he couldn't hold back any longer. He thrust inside her tight heat, feeling the walls of her pussy and the cream spilling from her with her orgasm.

She went over the edge, and seconds later Lash joined her, growling out her name as his seed filled her.

For a few seconds, he hoped she fell pregnant and he'd have a reason to keep her close to him for the rest of his life.

Slamming his lips down on hers, he claimed her pleasured cries and basked in what they meant.

Chapter Ten

Lash collapsed on top of her. Angel wrapped her arms around his back, stroking his skin. She was tired yet not. It was really strange how she was feeling. From the look of the world outside the sun was rising up in the sky, but she wasn't ready to go to sleep. Lash had made love to her. She knew he hadn't fucked her because she'd seen what fucking was all about in the club. What she'd shared with Lash had nothing to do with that and everything to do with making love.

She pushed those thoughts to the back of her mind. There was no chance of a loving future with Lash. He wasn't the type of man to settle down, and she couldn't handle a future with worrying about what he was up to. She could already see herself pacing the house, checking the clock wondering if he was fucking someone else and he'd come to her when he was done.

Pushing those thoughts out of her mind as well, Angel just allowed herself the luxury of stroking his body. She pictured the tattoo on his back and smiled. He was the first man to ever make her feel small and delicate.

"I'll move in a second. I just need some time to get feeling back into my body," he said, kissing her shoulder.

Angel giggled. She couldn't help herself.

"Was I that good?" she asked.

"You've no idea how amazing that was." Lash leaned up and looked down at her. In one swift move he changed their positions so she was on top and he was on the bottom.

"I'm never going to get used to that," she said.

"What?"

"You being able to move me so easily. I'm not used to it." She tucked some hair behind her ear and smiled down at him. "However, I could get used to being on top." Straddling his waist with his cock still deep inside her, Angel sat up. She traced his muscles and the lines of his tattoos. His skin was darker for being outside more. Her hands were incredibly pale in comparison.

"You made me proud tonight," he said, reaching up to cup her breast.

She let out a moan when he pinched her nipple. The action sent a new wave of lust straight to her core.

"When?"

"When you danced on the table with Tate."

"I thought you were angry with me dancing?" She hadn't been so drunk she'd forgotten what was going on. The whiskey had given her the courage to have a good time. Talking with Tate and watching everyone have fun she'd wanted to be like them for at least once in her life. Her mother hadn't wanted her to get involved with the bikers and did everything she could to keep her away.

Getting to know The Skulls had shown they were a bunch of guys with their own code. Lash wasn't mean or evil. He simply didn't live to what society expected. She was starting to see the thrill of it. Lash had explained what the club was really all about, and part of her wanted in. She didn't want them to judge her when so many had. Her name alone was enough to make people start to assume things about her.

Fortunately, Lash had taken care of her little problem.

"I didn't hate your dancing, baby. I loved your dancing. I was proud because you were dancing for yourself and with Tate."

"I don't know what you mean?" she said, confused.

"The sweet-butts dance to entice and to draw the guys in. You weren't looking for any attention. I saw it in your eyes. The only thing you were interested in was letting go. It's the same for Rose. She doesn't dance for Hardy or to tease the guys. She dances because she loves it." His hands settled on her hips.

"I thought guys preferred it when a woman teased," Angel said. He was right though. Getting up on the tables, she hadn't been thinking about who was going to watch her or how they were going to view her. She'd gotten up to dance.

"We like to be teased, but there's also something about a woman who doesn't give a fuck about anyone else. You closed the guys off, and it was like the only people who existed to you were you and Tate. There was no expectation from the guys, and your innocence added to the whole package."

Lash tightened inside her. Arching her back she let out a moan as an answering pulse spread throughout.

"If you keep doing that, baby, I'm going to fuck you again."

"What's wrong with that? You've already taken me once," she said, grabbing his hands when they made to retreat from her body.

"If we don't stop and give you chance to rest you're going to be sore."

She squealed as he picked her up in his arms, sliding his cock out of her body.

"I wouldn't mind, Lash," she said. He dumped her on the bathroom floor, and she watched him start to fill the bathtub. Folding her arms she let out a groan not wanting him to wash her or anything. If he cleaned her it would feel very medieval, and she wasn't ready for that.

"I would mind. A little soaking and tenderness now means later I can fuck you until my heart's content."

She was too busy admiring his ass to hear him. "What?"

He looked at her over his shoulder. "Make no mistake, Angel, I'll be fucking you every chance I get, and I'm looking forward to every second of it. You'll take me as well."

"What do you mean?" she asked.

"It means that if I want you, you'll take me. If that place is in the car, outside, the toilet, I don't care, you'll submit to me." He helped her to her feet, his hands fisted her hair, and he bruised her lips with a punishing kiss. "You're mine, Angel. My woman to fuck, take care of, and cherish."

She noticed he didn't use the word love. Angel tried not to be disappointed, but a small sharp sting pierced her heart at his lack of use of the word.

Angel responded to his kiss though the disappointment threatened to have her in tears. She pushed them aside along with all of her other thoughts. For once she'd be happy with the here and now rather than becoming depressed thinking about the future. If Lash wasn't in her future then Fort Wills was not. She'd leave before she had to put up with him sleeping with all kinds of different women.

He broke the kiss once again. "You're making me lose all my control. I just want to fuck you." He growled then picked her up in his arms.

Lash lowered her into the warm water and moved her forward so he could sit behind her. The bath was filled with lavender scented bubbles. He pushed her hair over one shoulder then settled back, bringing her back against him.

"How does it feel?" he asked, whispering against her neck.

"Perfect. It feels really nice." Her pussy did feel a little tender, and she was pleased he'd stopped her from going again. "Have you taken many virgins?" she asked, teasing.

"No, you're my first, and I won't be doing it again."

She recalled fighting him. When he'd pierced inside her flesh she hadn't known what to do. The pain had been so immense she didn't know how she was going to survive having him inside her.

"I'm sorry for fighting you," she said.

"I'm not sorry." He kissed her shoulder. "If I ever hurt you like that I want you to fight back. Never take the pain, Angel."

His arm wrapped around her middle. She covered his hand and chuckled as he sneaked under the water to stroke her pussy.

"I thought you were waiting until I felt better."

"I'm giving you pleasure. I'm not fucking you again for at least a day, and after that, you're mine."

He kissed her head, stroking her pussy at the same time. "Open your legs wider," he said, instructing.

"How? There's nowhere for me to go?"

"I don't give a shit about water on the floor. I can clean it up. Lift your legs over the edge."

Rolling her eyes, she did as he commanded and rested her legs over either side of the bath, opening her up. The warmth of the water made her gasp as it touched her exposed pussy.

"That's it, I can find you easily now." His finger slid between her slit, down to her core. She cried out when his thick finger penetrated her.

"I thought you weren't going to penetrate," she said, gasping.

"I'm not penetrating you with my cock, but you can take my finger." He pumped inside her adding a second finger. His thumb grazed her clit making her tighten on his digits. There was no stopping the need burning inside her. She needed him so much.

"Ride my fingers, baby. When you're ready I'm going to fuck your pussy so much you're going to wonder how you stayed a virgin for so fucking long." His breath whispered across her neck.

Moaning, Angel closed her eyes thrusting up to meet his fingers. It felt so good having him inside her. His two fingers were not as big as his cock, and she was thankful for that. Lash was right about not having sex again. Her pussy was tender, and she wouldn't be able to handle another fucking.

What about Lash?

Opening her eyes she realised he was going without any touching.

Reaching behind her she gripped his fat cock and started working the shaft.

"What are you doing?" he asked, nibbling her neck.

"We can't have sex, but I can give you just as much pleasure as you're giving me." She met him stroke for stroke and worked her palm over his erection.

His caresses increased, and she rode the wave of her orgasm at the same time as bringing him to release.

Lash growled against her neck as they came together. Her head pounded, and she cried out.

They were both sweating and gasping for breath when they came down.

"We're going to need to change the water," he said, kissing her more.

"Why?"

"I've just come, baby, and unless you want to wash in cum we need to change the water."

She laughed. "How about we shower and get back to bed?" she asked, wanting him back on the bed.

"Deal."

****

On Sunday morning Lash woke up to Angel curled naked around him. They'd spent all day Saturday exploring each other, sleeping and eating when they remembered. Angel was insatiable, and Lash truly believed he'd found his soul mate in life and in the bedroom.

Running his hand down her back he gazed down at her sleeping face. She looked so peaceful.

The sound of his cell phone ringing in the distance made him curse. Untangling himself out from under her body Lash padded naked out of his bedroom and down to where he'd tossed his cell phone the day before.

"What?" he asked, answering the call.

"I thought you'd be happy to hear from us," Tiny said.

Glancing at the clock, Lash saw it was close to noon. Cursing, he walked into the kitchen and started firing up some coffee. "I've been busy."

"Angel that good?"

"Don't start." Annoyance gripped him at Tiny's teasing. "Do I need to remind you of Tate and how she's only going to get worse?" Lash asked.

"Tate is why I'm calling. We need to make a move," Tiny said.

"What do you mean?" Lash tensed wondering what he'd missed in the day he'd been away.

"Our source has let us know they're gunning for Tate and the women. They're going to make a move in the next week or so. The men are moving their women out of the way and sending them away." Tiny stopped to curse.

"What? What is it?"

"We can't move Angel and Tate," Tiny said.

Lash frowned. "I don't get it. If the women are a threat then why are we leaving two of them behind?"

"If we get rid of them the Lions will know we're on to them. There's nothing we can do about it, Lash. I'm upping the protection, and the Prospects are armoured up. No harm will come to our women."

"I don't like this," Lash said.

Thinking about anything happening to his woman made it hard for Lash to function.

"I've warned Tate, and she's agreed to stay out of trouble. I was thinking you could take Angel to be with her. We'll be on the lookout. The women don't know what's going on, and I want to keep it that way."

Lash rubbed fingers through his hair. "How are we going to handle this?" The Lions were threatening their turf, but they hadn't killed any of their members. The only problem was Angel's father. He was the one selling out information. The stupid bastard didn't realise the danger he was putting his daughter and town in.

"We're taking David out and killing most of the Lions. I've warned the sheriff, and he's going to be on call in case we need him to break it up."

Lash didn't feel comforted about the law being on his case. In fact it irritated him. The law in Fort Wills didn't handle the true problems. They sat on their asses eating donuts and pretending they took care of business.

The Skulls kept the shit off the streets. The Skulls made sure the town was safe, and yet there were some of the locals who despised them.

Shaking his head, Lash looked up to see Angel leaning against the doorframe. Her hair was messy, and her whole body shouted out that she'd been fucked good.

"I know you hate this plan, but this is what we do. We don't bring shit to Fort Wills. The Lions are our only threat, and we'll handle it outside of town, away from the women." Tiny sounded tired.

"Are you okay?" Lash asked, gesturing for Angel to come closer.

"I'm fine."

"Eva?" Lash figured the only person to leave Tiny feeling tired and fed up was the young nanny.

"Is there anyone else I'd let do this to me?"

He didn't answer. Lash doubted Eva knew the power she had over the big, scary biker.

"I want you here as soon as you can. Nash is brooding, and Kate's not helping him."

Rolling his eyes Lash agreed to stop by when he could. It was Sunday, and he was staying with Angel for as long as he could.

He hung up the cell and wrapped his arms around his woman. "Good morning," he said.

"Morning." She rested against him. "Who was on the phone?"

"Tiny, club stuff."

"I hope Tate's not in trouble for her turning up at the party."

"He'll be pissed, but he won't do anything."

Lash cupped her between her thighs and moaned when he felt her dripping flesh. "Are you still sore?"

"No, I've not been sore for a long time." Angel moaned, opening her thighs wider.

"Bend forward," he said, lust replacing any concern he'd originally had. He needed her so fucking bad.

She braced her arms on the counter, turning her head to look at him over her shoulder. "Will it always be like this?"

"I fucking hope so," Lash said, running a hand down her back. He opened the cheeks of her ass wide to see her puckered hole and the creamy slit of her pussy.

Running his fingers through her cream he penetrated her with two fingers before sliding them back to her anus. Angel moaned around him.

Lash shut out all of the problems that was occurring in his life and settled his focus on Angel.

"I'm going to fuck this ass real soon, baby. You'll let me, won't you?" he asked.

"Yes, anything you want."

He smiled. With his other hand he grabbed his aching cock and pressed the tip to her entrance. He'd gone without her cunt for a day, and he was already close to the edge. When the tip of his cock was inside her, Lash grabbed her hips with both hands and slammed inside her.

They both cried out, and Lash smiled as her pussy rippled around him. She was soaking wet, and he wouldn't have her any other way. "You're so tight."

Her hands were flat on the surface, and Lash was free to touch her at his will.

"Lash, please."

"There's no pain this time is there, baby?" he asked. He didn't move and ran his hands all over her ass and back.

"No, there's no pain. It feels so good."

Opening the cheeks of her ass, Lash watched his cock slide out of her body and then glide in. Her cunt took every inch of him.

Slapping her ass, he gripped her waist and then rammed inside of her for the next few thrusts. She took him, her hands holding onto the counter.

He took it in turns between looking at the side of her face and where he disappeared inside her warm heat.

"How does it feel?" he asked, slipping a hand around to her pussy. Lash stroked her wet pussy, finding her clit and pinching it.

"Amazing."

Caressing her with two fingers Lash felt her pussy respond by gripping him tight. Letting out a growl, he fingered her pussy until a stream of cum soaked his cock. She cried out, riding his fingers and cock.

"That's it, baby, ride me."

He slapped her ass loving the sight of his hand print on her ass. Once all the shit with the Lions was out of the way he was getting his name printed on her flesh. He wanted everyone to know who his woman belonged to.

"Lash." She screamed his name as another climax gripped her.

"Who do you belong to, baby?"

"You, always you."

"Say it. Say you belong to me." He gripped her hips and pounded inside her heat. Lash was rough, and he didn't care. He needed to feel her submit to him and say the words.

"I belong to you, Lash."

A wave of peace floated around him, calming him.

"Tell me no other man is going to feel your warmth."

"Lash?"

"Fucking say it, and mean it?"

"There's never going to be any other man. It's you, Lash. It will always be you."

Groaning, Lash let himself go, and the release washed over him. Slamming inside Angel's body he let himself go.

With a final thrust he erupted inside her. Rubbing her ass Lash came back to his senses and saw Angel looking at him over her shoulder. Her green eyes made him pause once more. He saw the question in her eyes, but instead of answering her, he ignored it and pulled out.

Glancing down he saw the puffy red of her bare lips and the white of his seed escaping.

All he wanted to do was hold him inside her body. The consuming need to bind her to him in some way, terrified him. Words didn't feel enough to him. He felt the need to have something that gave him a reason to always be in her life. A baby would guarantee that. Shaking his head, he rinsed out a towel and pressed it to her pussy.

"That was the best way I've ever woken up on a Sunday." He dropped a kiss to the cheek of her ass and smiled when she moaned.

"I thought you'd have plenty of women to satisfy your cravings."

"Only when I was at the club. I don't bring women here. This is my space."

He poured two coffees, grabbed two bowls and the only box of cereal he kept. Lash quickly poured her a bowl. Setting everything on the table, Lash pulled her into his lap to eat.

"But I'm here," she said, cutting into his thoughts.

"What?" he asked, frowning.

"You said you never bring women here, but I'm here and I'm a woman."

"You're *my* woman, Angel. It's different."

She didn't say anything more, which he was thankful for. After breakfast he phoned one of the other Prospects to stay inside the house while he was at the bar.

Angel smiled at him when he left, and he wished he could tell her what she wanted to hear. Until he was sure the threat of the Lions was gone, he wasn't going to get her hopes up.

LASH

Chapter Eleven

Over the next couple of days Angel was confined to the house or the club when Lash needed to go and be with his crew. She didn't mind being around him at all. Her feelings for Lash had intensified, and she no longer doubted if she loved him. Angel knew she was in love with Lash, which meant his secrets made it hard for her to handle. She knew he was keeping something from her, and she hated it. Secrets, no matter who kept them, were always bad things. She hated secrets. Look what happened to her father when he'd kept secrets from her.

Other than being confined and the secrets, everything else was amazing. When Lash gave her his full attention all of her doubts vanished. He was so attentive, insatiable, and he rocked her world. She never thought it was possible to be walking on cloud nine, but her life had turned into a constant cloud nine whenever she was with Lash. Angel never thought Lash could be so giving and fun. He bought plenty of DVDs for them to watch, and they were not always action flicks or horror movies.

She'd lost count of the number of times he'd cooked for her, not just breakfast but dinner and dessert. They talked about everything, apart from the club. Angel understood talking about the club was off limits, and she didn't mind. The less she knew about his dealings inside The Skulls, the happier she was.

Her thoughts turned to their intimate time together. She couldn't call it fucking or just sex. What they shared together was something more than sex and fucking. When they were together, exploring and making love, she felt connected to him. They were equals, and she gave pleasure as much as received it.

He'd also started playing with her ass. She knew he wanted to take her *there,* but she couldn't help but hold some reserves about it. Anal sex terrified her, even though she'd snuck on the internet to check out some of the links.

Angel was sure Lash knew she'd checked out some sites because when he came out of his office the other day he'd smirked at her. He'd not said anything embarrassing, but he'd pulled her close and kissed her head. She didn't know what it was about him kissing her temple, yet she found it to be one of the sweetest things he'd ever done.

Rubbing her temple she listened to Tate moan over the phone. "I mean he's got Steven here all the time. He's got his own bloody room and everything. Eva and I have been banned from going out. Dad completely freaked out yesterday when Eva took out the trash. He yelled, she screamed at him, and it ended with him slamming the office door and Eva locking herself in her room. I swear I'm going to lock them in a room and make them get over their issues."

"Tiny's protecting both of you. I don't know what from, but I'm not allowed out without Blaine. He's always here. Lash told me he's the next best Prospect." Angel rubbed her hands down her thighs.

Blaine was in the kitchen making another coffee for them both. They were playing cards, and he'd given her some privacy to make her phone call.

"Dad is going to drive Eva away. I know he is. I've seen her looking at other job vacancies. I can't blame her. I love her like a Mom, but she's only my nanny. I'm too old to have a nanny," Tate said. "So, anyway, how are things going with the stud muffin? I've heard he can be a bit of an animal, which is totally gross because I see him as a brother, but I'm trying to be supportive."

Laughing, Angel smiled at Blaine as he brought their coffees through. "He's perfect. I can't fault him, and I'm not going to go into details, Tate. He's like a brother to you, and I'm not keen on telling you everything."

"Spoil-sport."

She heard Tate sigh.

"I can't stand this. I want to see you. I know it has only been a couple of days since I've last seen you, but I need some more company. Eva would like to meet you as well."

Angel glanced at the clock on the far wall. "I'll talk with Lash when he gets home. He should be back around seven."

"Tell him I'll go bat-shit crazy if he says no," Tate said.

"Did anyone ever tell you that you sound like a spoiled biker princess?" Angel asked.

"Do I look like the kind of woman who cares?"

Angel said not, but she believed Tate cared a whole lot. There were times she detected the vulnerability inside the other woman. Tate had been hurt in the past, and she was putting on a bullshit exterior to keep people out.

"I better go. Daddy's back, and he sounds in a foul mood again. Take care, Angel."

"And you."

She rang off and stared at Blaine, who was looking at his cell phone. "Are you okay?" she asked.

"Yeah, how's Tate?" he asked, pocketing his cell.

"She's not doing good at all. Do you think Lash will let me visit with her?"

He shrugged, taking a sip of his coffee. "I can't say."

All the members were silent.

"What about the other women? Are they confined at home or not?"

Blaine looked uncomfortable.

"What? What is it?" she asked.

"The old ladies have gone away. The guys have sent them away, but the sweet-butts are camping out at the club. Then there's you and Tate. I don't know what's going on."

His words sent pain throughout her whole body. The old ladies were gone, which could only mean she was not an old lady. Was she reading the wrong signals from Lash? Did he want to get rid of her?

She wanted to grill Blaine more, but Lash walked through the front door. Closing her eyes she waited for him to come into the room. His hand went to her shoulder, and he kissed her temple once again.

"Hey, baby, missed me?"

Her body heated like it always did whenever he was close by. She couldn't stop her natural reaction to him. More than anything she wished she could stop the yearning deep inside.

"Yes, I missed you." There was no point in lying. She did miss him. He was the one person she thought of all the time. From the moment she went to sleep 'til when she woke up, her thoughts were consumed by him.

"You're free to go back to the club," he said, talking to Blaine.

"Sure thing. It was lovely playing, Angel."

Blaine made his way out of the house. Angel stayed sat on the sofa. She felt like she couldn't move.

"Do you want a stir-fry tonight?" Lash asked.

"Sounds lovely." She didn't know what to do.

Getting up from her seat she followed him into the kitchen.

"Are you okay?" he asked, when she took a seat opposite him. She sipped at her coffee and watched him work.

"I'm fine."

He frowned at her but started working. They didn't speak, which was a first. Lash made dinner, and afterwards she washed the dishes. Her actions were slow. On her way upstairs, Lash pulled her into his arms. Her body fired up ready for him.

"What's going on?" he asked.

Staring into his eyes, Angel couldn't hold it back.

"What am I to you?" The words left her without any other thought. She couldn't pull them back into her mouth. Angel stood, waiting for him to speak.

"What do you mean?" His gaze came through narrowed slits.

"Well, I'm not a sweet-butt because I'm not fucking everything in sight, and yet I'm not an old lady because all of them have been sent on their merry way. What am I to you? Am I a fuck? Some entertainment? Or is this how my father is earning off the interest?" she asked, yelling. Hands on hips she glared at him and then was shocked as he raised his hand in the air.

He looked ready to commit murder. "I've never hit a woman out of anger, but right now you've pushed me to the edge. Don't you ever accuse me of fucking treating you like a whore." Lash pressed her against the wall. His hands slammed against the wall on either side of her head.

She tensed, shocked by his sudden rage.

"If the club was going to take interest out on you, baby, you'd be on a table spread out all day without anything in the way. We'd take our interest out any way we wanted, and you wouldn't ever rest." He moved closer until he was only a breath away. "We've done it before when the woman wanted all of us. We've taken out the interest on her body. You're not like that, and I would never let that happen, Angel. I called in the debt, and I was the one who claimed you."

Angel frowned. "What?"

"I was the one who called the debt in. Your father was getting in too deep, and I knew it was only a matter of time before he brought you down with him. I couldn't let that happen. You were always supposed to be mine." Lash cupped her cheek, caressing the skin down to her collarbone. "That what makes you different, baby. You're mine, and when people speak of you, you'll be known as Lash's woman."

His hands went down to her waist, pulling her close.

In the next instant his lips were on her, and Angel was melting once again.

"Never, ever, think of yourself as a whore or anything else. You're my woman, Angel, and that is all I can tell you for now."

"Why?" she asked.

"Because that's the way it's going to be. This is how it's going to be. There will be times when I have no choice but to keep stuff to myself. It has nothing to do with you. This is just the life I lead, and I can't bring you into it."

"How can I support you if you can't talk to me?" she asked. His words had soothed her concerns for the moment. She knew it was only a matter of time before insecurity reared its ugly head.

"I can talk to you. Knowing I never have to come with you with business is good enough for me. You're everything else I need, Angel. Please, support me by being you and not caring about the shit I do." He kissed her several times before looking at her. "Can you do that for me?"

"Yes, I can."

"Thank you." He tugged at her clothes, getting her naked and pushed her underneath him on the bed.

She gasped as he slid deep inside her. His thick cock pulsed and slid deeper still.

Was she weak for accepting whatever Lash would give her?

****

Tomorrow morning Lash was going to have a word to Blaine about saying stuff to his woman. The threat of the Lions was the only reason he wasn't making a deeper commitment. He wouldn't make a life-long commitment only to put it at risk with what was going down between the two clubs. So far no lives had been lost, but he couldn't always guarantee it.

Pushing the club and all worries out of his mind, Lash basked in the heat of her pussy as she surrounded him. This was what he wanted to come home to, a woman who wanted him as much as he wanted her. Angel was the love of his life. There were no doubts in his mind. He was totally in love with her.

"You're mine, baby," he said, pulling out of her tight warmth only to slam back inside.

"Yes." She reached up to caress his face. "And you're mine."

He fucked her hard against the bed wanting more. Leaving her warmth, he turned her onto her knees and brought her ass up in the air. He eased into her hot cunt, watching her take all of him without any pain.

She was always ready and waiting for him. He was addicted to her tight heat.

"Lash, um, more," she said.

Staring down at the puckered entrance of her ass, Lash knew he was going to claim that. He'd been waiting patiently, and he was running out of patience. Leaning over the bed, he grabbed the tube of lube.

Working plenty onto his fingers he pressed them to her ass. Sliding in two fingers, he fucked her pussy at the same time as working her ass to open to him.

Angel moaned, pressing back on him.

"That's it, baby, ride my cock and hands. I'm going to fuck you so hard, you'll be begging for more."

Stretching her tight ass open, Lash applied more lubrication to his shaft. He left her cunt and pressed the tip to where his fingers had just been. Lash watched himself disappear inside her ass an inch at a time.

"Does it feel good?" he asked.

"Yes." She moaned again, and he chuckled.

Gripping her hips, Lash sank to the hilt inside her ass. He stayed still giving her time to adjust to his cock in her ass. She was tighter than he'd imagined she would be.

"Are you ready for me to move?"

"Yes."

He eased out of her ass and slowly glided back inside her. His movements were slow, and he didn't rush. Part of anal sex was taking the time to enjoy it. Lash was hit square in the face by the knowledge he was all of Angel's firsts. He was the first guy to kiss her, to suck her pussy, and to fuck her. He'd claimed her mouth, ass, and cunt.

Yep, Angel was now his woman. He didn't find the revelation boring. In fact, he wanted to do everything with her over and over again.

Sliding deep inside her Lash closed his eyes letting himself absorb every single sensation. Her ass tightened around him in a little flutter. Biting on his lip he waited for her to calm down before moving again.

When he couldn't stand it anymore he changed positions.

"I want to kiss you," he said, taking her to the side with her back to him. His cock remained deep in her ass as he settled behind her. Gripping her cunt with one hand and her breast with another, Lash slammed his lips down on hers. He rode her body while holding onto her.

She was perfect for him. He was never afraid of hurting her. Angel took everything he gave her without complaint.

"Tell me you want it," he said, breaking the kiss and staring into her eyes.

"What?"

"Tell me you want me to come in your ass."

Her cheeks got even deeper in colour with his words.

"Say it, baby. I want to hear you say it."

She nibbled her lip. He pinched the bud of her clit and watched her squirm with pleasure.

"Say it."

"Come in my ass, Lash. Claim me."

He held her tight against him, took her lips, and brought her to orgasm in his arms. Only when she'd come did he allow himself the release of an orgasm.

Lash spilled his release inside her. His head thumped from the pounding of his blood. He tightened his grip around her holding her close. Kissing her head, neck, and lips, Lash knew he was never going to let her go.

"You're my woman, Angel. You'll never leave my side or my bed. You're mine."

She nodded but didn't say anything. They lay on the bed. The only sound to be heard was their uneven breathing.

"You've just fucked my ass," she said.

"And I'll be taking it again. You better get used to it, baby. I'm not giving you up," he kissed her lips staring down into her green eyes. "What?" he asked, seeing her need to speak.

"Will you be giving up the other women? The ones at the club who are easy and want you?"

He saw the jealousy in her eyes. Lash wasn't annoyed. He was fucking happy to see the jealousy shining in her eyes.

"Baby, I've not had any of those women in over a year. You're my one and only woman."

"Promise."

"It's a lifetime guarantee."

Lash kissed her once more and then untangled himself from her body. He picked her up in his arms. She protested, and he ignored her. He carried her through to the bathroom. Turning on the shower he waited for the water to get warm before tugging her inside with him.

"You're always so bossy," she said.

"It's a biker trait."

She rolled her eyes, letting him wash her body. "I feel like a doll."

"You know there are women out there who'd love a man to do shit like this. I made a mess, and I'm washing you. Stop moaning." He slapped her ass loving the sound of her squeal.

"You're always bad," she said.

"Better believe it."

She stayed silent as he soaped her body. He got her to lean against the wall as he washed away his leaking seed from her ass. Lash used cleaning her as an excuse to touch her. He couldn't take his hands off her. Her soft body called to him.

"Can I ask you a question?" she asked.

"Sure."

"Tate is sounding a little pissed with being confined to her home. She wants me to ask if I can go and visit her."

He chuckled. Tate wouldn't be the type of woman to ask, and he said so.

"She may have threatened to go bat-shit crazy on your ass, but I thought asking nicely would help first."

Lash spun her around to face him. He pressed his lips against hers. "Do you like Tate?"

She nodded. "Yeah, she's wonderful. She seems sad though."

"What do you mean?" He started to soap her hair as she spoke.

"The attitude seems a barrier to keep people out as if she's been hurt before. I find it sad."

He stared at her. She was an observant one. "Tate has been hurt in the past. She was close to one of the members, and he left her and the club. It was a horrid betrayal."

"Murphy?"

"Yeah, his real name is Dillon James. She fell for him hard. He was the Prospect who saw her to high-school and was her date for the prom. I think Tiny only kept him a Prospect for so long because Tate liked him. Once you're a member you don't do babysitting duties unless you have to," Lash said. "They grew close, and there was a time after he left when Tate went a little crazy."

"Crazy, how?"

"She wouldn't eat and tried to push everyone away. I prefer the attitude to the tears and pain. She's fighting now whereas before she was letting go."

"Poor Tate. I knew something had gone on between her and Murphy from our time at the mall, but I didn't think it was that."

Lash shrugged. "Tiny does what he can, but he can't fix her broken heart."

They finished off their shower, and Lash took her back to bed.

"So can I go and see her?" Angel asked.

"I'll talk to Blaine and arrange it."

"Thank you." Angel kissed him and then settled down. Within seconds she was asleep, and Lash took the time to watch her sleep.

He knew it was only a matter of time before the Lions made their move, and he hoped to God that Tiny knew what he was doing.

Chapter Twelve

After seeing Lash off to the club Angel had finished her breakfast while Blaine made some calls on his cell phone. She was going to see Tate today, and she was waiting for Blaine to be ready to take her.

Sipping her hot coffee she watched the other man talk in the cell phone. He looked relaxed and was smiling. When he was finished he turned back to her, smiling.

"Are you ready to go?" he asked.

"Yeah, who were you speaking to?" She cringed at the invasion of privacy. "I'm sorry, I shouldn't have asked."

"No, it's okay. I was talking to my daughter," he said, smiling. He pulled a wallet out of his back pocket and handed her a photo.

"You're a father?" she asked, taking the photo and seeing a smiling blonde looking back at him. The little blonde was in the arms of a raven-haired woman.

"Yeah, that's my baby girl, Darcy, and my woman, Emily." He cleared his throat. She handed back the wallet. "They're both beautiful women."

"They are. Emily won't let me see my daughter at the moment. I've had a rough few years. The club has really helped me out. I know I'm an old Prospect at twenty-five, but they're my world. I'll do anything for them."

Angel smiled. "I hope you figure things out soon."

"So do I. Are you ready to go?" Blaine asked.

"Yeah." They headed out to the car. "Do you mind if I ask how old Emily is?"

The woman in the photo looked young.

Blaine went red. "She's eighteen in the photo, and she's just turned twenty."

"Did you…?" She couldn't finish. Had he slept with a minor?

"No, Emily was eighteen when we were together. I would never do that. I fucked up, not Emily. She needed me, and I wasn't there. It's my fault, no one else."

Angel nodded. "I'm sorry. You're the first person to give me any details of their life."

"No problem. I've been told I need to talk about my family."

They climbed in the car, and Blaine headed toward Tate's home. Angel pressed the button to call Tate to let her know they were on their way.

Tate didn't answer the phone, and Angel tried her number again.

"I'm pleased you've told me. It must be hard having a family and not seeing them."

"It can be," Blaine said, agreeing.

"Do Emily and Darcy live in town?"

"Yeah. She doesn't want anything to do with me. I can't do anything about it. She's got full custody and is an amazing mother."

Angel smiled. When she couldn't get Tate a third time she left it alone, figuring her friend was too busy to answer the phone.

The rest of the drive was peaceful. Blaine talked about his little girl and how advanced she was. Several times Angel rested her hand against her stomach wondering if she was pregnant. Lash never wore a condom with her. She probably should make him and get tested or something, but she trusted him.

Shaking her head, they pulled into the driveway of Tate's home. She saw Steven's bike and was thankful Blaine would have someone to talk to.

They walked around back. Tate had told her to always walk around the back. She let herself in the back door. The kitchen was silent.

"Tate, honey, we're here. I finally talked Lash into letting me come." They rounded a corner, and Angel froze.

Steven was on the ground, a pool of blood around him. Tate was stood with her arms out in surrender. Tears were spilling from her cheeks as she looked at the man in front of her. Angel didn't recognise him, but she saw Murphy at the back of the group.

Blaine tried to pull her out of the way. He was pulling a gun out of his pocket. It was too late.

Two shots were fired, and Angel felt his grip loosen. He fell to the floor at her feet. Tate screamed, and Eva was jerked. Angel stared at the man at her feet. She'd been getting to know him. He was a father and turning his life around.

Going to her knees she stared at his chest and stomach. Blood was oozing out of holes. Tears sprang to her eyes.

"No, this can't be happening." She pressed her hands to the wound trying to stem the blood flow.

"Please," he said, coughing.

Someone grabbed her arm tugging at her.

"Leave me alone!" She screamed, pulling away and going to Blaine.

"I'm sorry," Blaine said.

Tears spilled down her cheeks. No, it was so unfair. He was making his life better. The club would fix him, and he'd get his happily ever after.

"Don't be sorry. This is not your fault." She applied more pressure to the wounds and cried as she felt the blood pooling out of the wound.

He reached in his pocket. "Tell … Emily … I'm sorry … I … was trying."

"Don't talk, Blaine. You're going to see her."

His eyes closed, and Angel didn't have time to check before she was pulled roughly to her feet.

"Get the fuck away from him. He's dead, bitch."

Angel didn't feel the pain from being pulled. She couldn't tear her gaze away from Blaine or from Steven. They were both Prospects, and yet they were dead at her feet like they were nothing. She'd gotten to know them both, and now they were dead.

Shoved against Tate, Angel stared at the men before her. She saw the Lion emblem, and instant hate consumed her.

"Why didn't you take the hint when I didn't answer the phone?" Tate asked, crying.

"I thought you were in the shower or something." She was numb. There were no other words to describe what she was feeling.

"I wish I was."

"Call your fucking father, bitch. Let him know that we've got this town, and his crew better stand in line or we'll fucking kill you."

Tate was handed a phone. Angel saw the other woman hesitate. She glanced at the back of the crew and saw Murphy staring at Tate. What she saw next terrified her. Her father was stood next to Murphy. His face was hard as if a mask had come over him. He glared at her but didn't say a word. Hatred filled her at the sight. Her own father was the one responsible for all this mess. He was betraying The Skulls, and she wished he didn't make it through this day. The bastard deserved to rot for what had just happened to Blaine.

"Make the call, Tate," Angel said.

Her hands were shaking as she squeezed her friend's hand. Glancing down she saw her hands were covered with red. Rubbing them down the skirt she wore, she tried to wipe Blaine's blood of her hands. How could he be dead? He was getting his life together.

Shaking her head, she listened to Tate as she said hello to her father.

The phone was loud enough for her to hear the conversation.

"Hello, Tate, honey, what's the matter?" Tiny asked.

"Dad, you need to come home. The … the Lions are here, and Steven's down. Blaine's down as well."

"Give me the phone, bitch." The guy in charge snatched the phone and started cursing down the phone.

"Are you happy now?" Tate asked. Her gaze was directed at Murphy.

Angel wrapped her arms around Tate, holding her close.

"Is this what you wanted, death? No wonder you wanted to go with the Lions, they're just fucking pigs in a jacket," Tate said. The man holding the phone backhanded Tate.

She got hurt in the process.

"I suggest you get your asses down here. We're going to end this, and then I'm taking your daughter, Tiny. She's got a smart mouth, but I know what to do with a smart mouth, bitch. Just ask the whores who work for me."

The phone was thrown to the floor and stamped on.

Angel went to her knees. She cupped Tate's face and saw her friend had a split lip. How she could see past the tears was beyond her.

"We'll get through this. Tate, look at me. We'll get through this."

"Your daughter's a dreamer, Marston."

She didn't let his words affect her. Holding Tate in her arms she saw Eva was let go. The other woman went to Tate's side.

"Come here, baby."

Even though there was less than ten years between the women, Tate curled up against Eva. "Your father will come, I promise."

For the next thirty minutes Angel sat on the floor with her legs folded waiting for the others to arrive. She never thought she'd be so relieved to hear the sound of bikes. Outside the front window she saw the shadows of the bikes crowd around. Letting out a sigh she held her breath as the front door was opened. Tiny, Lash, Nash, Butch, Zero and several of the other bikers including Hardy entered the house. Angel realised the shit was going down in Tiny's house. If this was her home, she'd be pissed. From the look on his face, Tiny was more than pissed. He was livid.

"You finally decided to turn up," the man said.

"We meet again, Jeff," Tiny said. "Tate, you okay?"

"Been better."

"Eva?" Tiny asked. His gaze never strayed from the man now known as Jeff.

"Fine."

Angel looked at Lash. His face was hard as he looked at her. Angel couldn't do anything to comfort him. She was in pain.

"Now, let me tell you how things are going to go. You're going to pack your shit up, and you're going to leave Fort Wills. This is Lion territory now. My land, my club, and you're going to get the fuck out of town," Jeff said. Her father was pulled to the front. "He's transferred all of your funds into my account. You're penniless. I've won."

There was silence at Jeff's demands, and then Tiny burst out laughing followed by the rest of the men.

"What's so fucking funny?" Jeff yelled at the room.

"You're so fucking stupid to think I'd trust that piece of shit with my money. David got fuck all other than what we fed him. In fact." Tiny held his hand out to the group. Nash handed him a piece of paper. "We've got everything from your club. Your money, which was very little, and we've bought your property, Jeff. You're gone, finished."

"What? How?" Jeff asked, looking startled.

"Do you really think we'd let David loose on our money? We've got cameras all around and to listen and to watch. We heard him make the deal with you. He's a sloppy guy, and it was easy to change everything he did."

Jeff turned to growl at David.

"I didn't think anyone was watching me," David said.

"You didn't even check. You fucking idiot."

"So, you're in my house, threatening my family, and you think you're going to walk away from that?" Tiny asked.

Angel watched as Jeff went angry. The Skulls were laughing at him, all because of David's sloppiness and greed. It felt like it was in slow motion, but Jeff moved to them. He kicked Tate out of the way and pointed a gun at Eva.

Silence rang out once more. "I see I've got your attention. How about I kill your nanny?"

The only way to describe the expression on Tiny's face was cold. It was like he grew frozen.

"I see I've got your attention."

"You've picked the wrong woman," Eva said. "I'm the working nanny. I'm not that important."

"Shut up, Eva," Tate said.

Angel screamed as another shot rang out. Eva slumped on the ground holding her chest. Jeff walked close to the other woman. Tiny was held back by his bikers.

"Let's see if you're right, honey. I think you mean more to Tiny than you think."

"Murphy, now!" Tiny roared the instruction, and all hell broke loose. Guns were fired, and Tate forced her to the floor. Angel covered her head, curling up as tight as possible as the fight rang out.

She didn't know how long the fight lasted. Her arm was touched, and when she turned around she saw Lash stood over her.

"We've got it covered, baby," he said.

Looking around her she saw several fallen bodies, but there were also some of the Lions standing. Wrapping her arms around his neck he helped her to stand. "They shot Blaine. He's hurt. We need to get him to the hospital," she said.

"We will. I promise."

Tiny had Jeff around the neck. "You fucking breathe in my direction again, and I'll fucking kill you."

"I'm just going to handle this," Lash said, stroking her cheek.

Angel nodded going to Tate. She was knelt over Eva who held her shoulder.

"I got shot," Eva said.

"I don't think it's inappropriate to ask for a raise," Tate said.

All three women chuckled. "I never expected so much excitement," Angel said.

Looking over her shoulder she saw Lash helping Tiny out. His brother was on the phone calling an ambulance. A couple of The Skulls were also checking to see if Blaine and Steven were alive. Out of the corner of her eye she saw her father stand to his feet. He held a gun in his hands, which he raised.

Acting on instinct, Angel went to her feet and ran toward Lash. The shot rang out, and pain exploded inside her chest. She collapsed to the floor, and all she heard was the dull beating of her heart.

****

Lash reacted. His woman had just been shot. He charged at her father, and the older man was no match for him. Lash was stronger, bigger, and he needed to hurt the man who'd hurt his woman. There was no stopping him. The room was washed in red, and it was all because of this man that there was so much blood.

Grabbing the man, he slammed his head against David's. He pummelled David's body with his fists, and then when he couldn't stand it anymore, Lash wrapped his hands around his neck and snapped.

He despised the violence, but he couldn't stop his actions. Lash watched David fall at his feet. Without waiting for the body to hit the ground he went to his knees beside Angel. Pulling her into his lap, he held her tight.

"Lash," she said. "It hurts."

"The ambulance is on its way. You stupid woman, you never step in front of a bullet." Tears filled his eyes, and for the first time since his parents died, Lash let the tears fall.

"I h-had t-to. He was going t-to s-shoot you."

He shook his head. The rest of the room faded against the pain of her bleeding out.

"You shouldn't have done it. I can take a bullet, but I can't lose you."

She smiled when she looked at him. "I love you."

His heart stopped beating. "What?"

"I love you, Lash. You're the only man for me."

Lash shook his head. "I love you, too, baby."

The paramedics crashed through the door, and they started working without even hesitating.

Angel was taken from him, and Lash forced his way into the back of the ambulance. He knew the others would join him at the hospital. For the trip he needed to make sure she made it. Holding her hand, he refused to back down even when the paramedic glared at him.

"Don't fucking think of ordering me about," Lash said, holding onto his woman.

She passed out, but Lash wouldn't let go. The trip to the hospital was fast, and only when he had to did he watch her be wheeled away. One of the nurses escorted him to a waiting room. He was covered in blood. Instead of cleaning the blood off, he sat in the seat waiting. The others in the room left him alone.

Within the hour Tiny along with Tate and the others turned up. Tiny and Tate looked pale as they took a seat next to him.

"They're operating on Eva. She passed out before they moved her to the ambulance, and the guy said they couldn't find a pulse," Tate said, sitting next to him. "Eva's strong, right? I mean, she can't die."

Lash sat forward, locking his bloodied fingers together. "Everyone can die, Tate." He thought about David. Shit, what was he going to do?

"Some of our men are taking care of the mess," Tiny said.

Glancing toward his leader Lash frowned. "You can't get rid of that mess, Tiny. I snapped Marston's neck."

Tiny glared at him. "As far as anyone's concerned nothing happened, and if it did, the Lions attacked us. I'm not losing one of my men to that scum, and that's the last of it."

Lash went to argue, but Tate pressed a hand to his leg silencing him. "Don't." She mouthed the words at him.

Hardy and Zero were sat next to the door. Lash imagined the others, including his brother, were taking care of business.

"So, Murphy never left The Skulls?" Tate asked.

Murphy had taken the role of being their spy. They'd made it look like a betrayal, but all the time Murphy was reporting back.

"He did what we asked, honey," Tiny said.

Tate nodded. Lash looked at the woman he regarded as a sister and saw she was only just holding it together.

"I need some coffee," Tiny said, standing to leave.

Within the hour the rest of the crew turned up. When Tate saw Murphy she stormed out.

Nash took the seat next to him. "Murphy hurt Tate."

"He left without any warning. She's hurting, but she'll get over it," Lash said.

"I hope you're right." Nash was silent for several minutes. "I took care of David. You're not going down for this."

"I may not have a choice," Lash said. "I killed a man."

"No, I lost two parents. I'm not losing you, Nigel. You're all I've got left, and I'm not letting you go down for him."

He looked at his brother. For Nash to call him by his real name, Lash knew he was fighting with his emotions.

"Okay, I'll try," Lash said.

"Good."

There was silence once again.

"So Angel's the one?" Nash asked.

"You must think it's crazy loving her and only wanting to be with her. She's my future, Nash. I love her, and I'd do everything to make her happy." Lash smiled, remembering her say that she loved him. He was going to hold her to it as well.

"No, crazy is fucking a woman you can't stand just so you could get the chance to see the woman you really wanted," Nash said.

Glancing at his brother, Lash saw the mask come off Nash. He saw his brother, and the pain was clearly written on his face.

"What do you mean?"

Nash shook his head. "I'm a fucking sucker. Kate has a sister. She's younger and sweet, and she doesn't look at the jacket or anything. I could never be with her, but when she talks to me, she talks to me. She refuses to call me Nash. I'm Edward to her." His brother laughed. "Can you believe I'm fucking a woman I can't stand just so I can see her?"

Lash stared at his brother shocked by the depth of emotion displayed.

"No, Lash, I don't think you're crazy. I think you're in love, and that I can understand."

"Mr. Myers?" A nurse came forward calling his name.

Standing up Lash faced the nurse. "That's me."

"Miss Marston is out of surgery and is awake. She's asking for you."

"What happened?" he asked.

"The bullet didn't touch her heart, but it was still in there. The surgeons have removed the bullet with minimal damage. She won't have the use of her arm for a few months."

Lash nodded and turned to his brother.

"Go on, go and see your woman."

Taking a deep breath he followed the nurse to his woman's room.

Angel lay in a large bed. Her face was pale, and her eyes closed. The nurse waved him on inside. Walking inside, her eyes opened, and she smiled at him.

"Hey," she said, reaching out with her good hand.

"Hey, yourself." He took her hand and sat beside her on the bed. Lash needed to be as close to her as possible.

"They told me I was going to make a good recovery."

"You ran in front of a bullet," Lash said. "Never, ever do that again."

"I couldn't have you shot, Lash." She looked down at their joined hands. "I'm in love with you, and I can't imagine life without you."

Cupping her face, he brought his lips down to hers.

"No, you do not, under any circumstances put yourself at risk for me, Angel." He kissed her again needing to taste her sweet skin.

"I understand," Angel said.

"I love you too much to lose you."

Her smile lit up her whole face. "You love me?"

"You have no idea how much I love you." He glanced down at the floor and cursed.

"What's the matter? What is it?" she asked. The concern was clear in her voice.

"I killed your father," he said, whispering to her.

"Good." There was no hesitation in her voice.

"Angel, I took his life. He's not coming back."

"I know, Lash. He was going to kill you. You don't understand. He didn't stop them when they were shooting people. He didn't help at all, and he caused all the problems. I don't care." She tightened her grip on his hand.

"I killed him."

"And your crew cleaned it up, right?" Angel asked.

"How do you know about that?"

"Rumours, and Tate likes to talk. I listen. You're not going down for killing him, Lash. He doesn't deserve your time. So it gets cleaned away, and we don't talk about it anymore, deal?"

"Deal."

He stared at her and wondered how she'd changed so fast. Lying down, Lash wrapped his arms around her.

"I love you, baby."

"I love you, too."

No one hurt his woman and got away with it. Angel was his woman, and he was happy for the whole world to know it. He was a Skull, and no one messed with a Skull and got away with it.

Chapter Thirteen

Angel stood behind Tate as she pinned up another balloon. It had been a couple of months since the shooting at Tiny's house, and they were finally welcoming home Steven and Blaine. Both men had been badly hurt with Blaine being in a coma for a couple of weeks. It had been touch and go for a few weeks, but fortunately they were both coming home for a party. She glanced across the bar to see Emily and Darcy playing in the corner. Everyone was pitching in for their welcome home party.

Twirling the ring on her finger she looked up to see Tate glancing down at her.

"You keep playing with your ring it's going to rub out," Tate said, climbing off the table.

A week after her coming out of the hospital, Lash had proposed. There was no way she'd turn him down. She'd screamed yes and then phoned Tate to tell her the good news. They were planning for a March wedding, which gave them enough time to organise everything. Lash wanted her to have a church wedding. She didn't care as long as she was with him.

"No, I'm not."

Arms wrapped around her waist pulling her close. "Leave her alone, Tate. She can play with her ring if she wants. It's hers." Lash kissed her neck. Letting out a moan, Angel leaned against him. He caressed her stomach as he kissed her neck and shoulder.

She watched Tate tense as Murphy stood next to her.

"I'm going to see if Mikey needs help with the booze." She smiled at Angel and moved away.

"She won't talk to me," Murphy said, watching her walk away.

"Tate's hurt, and it's going to take some time for her to get over that."

Murphy shook his head. "I don't know. She's closed off even from Eva and Tiny."

Angel wasn't about to ruin the party by telling them Tate was moving out of Tiny's home and into an apartment. She'd asked Tate to tell her father, but the other woman continued to refuse.

"She'll come around," Lash said, pulling Angel away.

"He looks sad," Angel said. They moved to the far wall, and Angel started to put more balloons and banners up.

"They'll get over it. I'm sure they'll figure it out."

Lash helped her finish the decorations, and when they got the sound of the horn they all crowded around waiting for the men to enter. Tiny had been the one to collect the men with Eva.

Angel leaned against Lash as they waited. His arms surrounded her with their warmth. The Skulls were her family now. She didn't miss her father at all. Any love she'd had for him died in the moments leading up to his death. She wished she could forgive him, but it wasn't possible. He'd grown greedy and put so many lives at stake because of it.

"I love you, baby," Lash said, whispering the words against her ear.

She smiled. Every time they made love Lash told her his true feelings. He opened up to her in ways she never thought possible.

"I love you, too."

The door opened, and they all erupted with cheers, laughter, and greetings.

Angel had asked for Emily and Darcy to wait in the kitchen. Moving forward she wrapped her arms around Blaine. "Are you okay?" she asked.

"I'm good. I, erm, I called Emily, but she didn't answer her phone."

In the last few months Angel had grown close to Blaine, and he was like a brother to her.

Taking hold of his hand she led him through the crowd and waited for Emily to exit. When she did Blaine looked shocked.

"She didn't answer her phone because she's been here waiting for you."

Angel had reached out to the other woman when Blaine survived the first few weeks after surgery.

"Blaine?" Emily said. Darcy was on her hip.

He turned to her. "Thank you," he said.

"Don't spoil it. Go and get your girls."

She watched him embrace both Emily and Darcy.

"You're a hopeless romantic," Lash said, muttering against her head.

Turning to face her man she wrapped her arms around his neck. "And you're complaining? I don't seem to recall you complaining when I made you a dinner and then sucked your cock for dessert."

"You're right. I like your romantic, dirty style."

Lash didn't leave her side for the remainder of the party. The sweet-butts avoided her while the old ladies embraced her.

Every now and then she saw Tate drinking from a bottle and walking around the club. Murphy was never far from her side.

Shaking her head, Angel knew she would deal with her friend another time. For now she was going to bask in having Lash in her arms.

"Come on, let's get out of here," he said.

She followed him outside. "You can't drive. You've had too much to drink."

"I don't need to drive."

He took her around the back of the club and farther into the woodland area. She'd never been this far away from the club before.

"Where are you taking me?" she asked.

Lash stopped and produced a blindfold. "It's a surprise."

Rolling her eyes, she waited for him to put the blindfold on, and he led her still farther away from the club.

"You're being all mysterious."

"From the movies you've put me through I'd say I was being romantic."

She chuckled.

After a few more minutes walking Lash stopped. He wrapped his arms around her waist and pulled her close. "I know you wanted to see Blaine when he came home, which is why I didn't stop you from going to the party, but I wanted to get you to myself."

The blindfold was removed, and Angel gasped. Candles were laid out around a blanket and what appeared to be a picnic basket.

"You planned a romantic picnic?" she asked. Tears filled her eyes.

"When it comes to you, baby, I plan everything." He helped her down to the blanket.

She sat and waited for him to dish out some of the food. "Did Tate help you with this?" she asked.

"And Rose and Eva. They wanted tonight to be perfect. You helped bring Blaine's woman back, and you saved me from being shot or worse. In your own unique way, Angel, you've won them all over. They love you for you," Lash said.

Kneeling in front of him she pulled him close for a kiss. "You always know what to say."

"Also, I wanted to show you something else."

Once all the food was laid out on the blanket, Lash stood. She watched, mouth watering, as he removed his shirt. "Look," he said, pointing at the tree.

Her gaze travelled down. Grabbing a candle she brought it close to his body. There, in the centre of his tree was her name. She gasped.

"When did you get this?" she asked. The flesh looked a little raw.

"I got it yesterday. I've been treating it, but you've been too preoccupied with the party to see. I'm pleased. I wanted you to see it at the right time."

"It's beautiful."

"Maybe one day you'll get your own tattoo?" he asked.

"I'd love to have your name on my skin."
****
Lash should probably tell her he'd already booked her an appointment, but he didn't want to upset her. She looked so happy gazing up at him. Dropping his hands to her face, Lash tilted her head back and brushed her lips with his.

She moaned, rubbing her body against his. "I love you, Nigel Myers."

He chuckled, groaning. "You're so not naming our children," he said.

"Why not? I'd be good at naming our children."

Running his hand down her body he cupped her ass, bringing her closer to his raging arousal. He was rock hard with the need to be inside her body.

"You didn't bring me here to seduce me. You brought me here to have sex," she said, smiling.

"Busted," Lash said, pushing her down until she lay spread out before him. He'd purposefully made her wear a skirt and top without anything on underneath. "Haven't you ever wanted to make love under the stars?"

"You're winning me over again."

"I'm wooing you."

"Woo me then."

Rearing back, he caressed her thighs and opened them as he did.

"That's cheating."

"I'm wooing you."

She chuckled, opening her thighs wider.

"You know you want me. I bet your pussy is soaking wet."

Angel didn't say anything. She was playing the game with him.

He moved down, pushed her skirt up and searched her pussy, finding her cream.

"I knew you'd be soaking wet." His fingers were drenched. She was clearly turned on. "You always do that to me." She moaned, thrusting up to meet his searching fingers. Lash pressed two fingers inside her and sucked her clit with his mouth. She cried out. Her fingers sank into his hair and pulled on the length.

"Feel so good," she said.

He nibbled and sucked on her clit, adding a third finger into her cunt.

"That's it, baby. Come for me." He released her long enough to speak.

"Please, Lash."

Pumping his fingers inside her, he stroked her tight nub feeling how close she was to the edge.

"Let go, Angel. I've got you. I've always got you." As he sucked her clit into his mouth, Angel exploded. Her cream gushed around his fingers, and he drank from her.

He continued to touch her with one hand while the other eased out his length. Lash got into position, aligned his cock, and thrust home.

Their moans combined and echoed on the night air.

"I love you, Angel."

Pulling out of her, Lash waited 'til only the tip was inside and then slammed in. He took her deep, prolonging her pleasure by teasing her clit.

"I love you, Lash. It will always be you."

Smiling, he made love to her, which had been his intention all along. The stars glinted around them. The candles cast a soft glow on her body. Lash had wanted everything to be perfect. He wanted her to remember this night for months and years to come.

When the pinnacle came, he cried out her name and collapsed on top of her. Angel shuddered around him. Her fingers caressed over his skin. Rolling to his side, he pulled Angel close.

"I never thought I could be this happy," she said.

"I don't think you imagined being engaged to a Skull, baby."

She chuckled, and the sound warmed his heart.

"No, I didn't imagine being engaged or having a future with a biker. You're all rough and hard, and you curse a lot."

"Fuck off," he said, joking.

Angel smiled up at him. "Mom said you guys were bad news, but that's not what I think."

"What do you think we are?" He brushed her chestnut hair off her face.

"I think you guys are one big family. You're not picture perfect and you'll never be the ideal, but you're a unit, a team, and a family. You can always depend on each other." She grabbed his hand and rested it against her stomach. "And that's what I'll want for our children, Lash."

He looked at her stomach and then at her. "Do you mean you're pregnant?" he asked.

Angel shook her head. "No, I'm not pregnant, Lash, but I want to be. I want to have your children and be your wife. Most of all I want to be your old lady and stand by your side."

His woman was tearing him up inside.

"Angel, you're the only woman I want by my side."

He kissed her lips, showing her with actions all the passion he held for her. They'd overcome so much in such a short time. Angel hadn't been affected by the death of her father, but he had. He'd kept the secret of his nightmares to himself. None of the crew knew he'd been affected by the death.

Taking a life with his bare hands had changed him in a fundamental way. He was strong, and knowing how strong had scared him. Snapping a guy's neck would stay with him forever. Angel hadn't judged him. She'd supported him and listened to him as he talked about his problems.

"Lash?"

"Yeah, baby?" he asked, staring up at the stars.

"Put a baby inside me."

His cock got instantly hard. All of his negative thoughts drifted away as he held Angel in his arms. Pulling off her clothes, Lash got her naked. They were going to be left alone for a long time. The party was still in full swing.

Pushing his jeans down his thighs, Lash gripped his erection once again. This time when he took her it would be different. Lifting her legs over his shoulder he seated himself to the hilt inside her. He didn't move at all. With his hands on either side of her head, he gazed down into her green depths.

He may be part of a biker club and that club may do questionable things from time to time, but in Angel's arms he felt like he could rule the world. His woman, his old lady, held the key to his happiness, and Lash was more than happy to bend to her will.

"I love you," he said, easing out of her slowly. Lash made love to her under a blanket of stars in the most perfect of ways.

Epilogue

Once Tate saw Angel and Lash leave, she grabbed her purse and headed out into the main parking lot. She wouldn't be going home today or any other day. Tate hadn't gotten around to telling Angel she'd signed the papers to her apartment. After twenty-three years of living under her father she was finally going to get away from him and away from The Skulls.

The only person she was interested in was Angel. They'd still be friends, but everything else was over. She was done with the secrecy, the betrayals, and a father who kept hurting a woman he was clearly in love with.

"Tate, wait!" Murphy shouted her name trying to slow her down.

And the last thing she was over with was Murphy, the backstabbing, lying, betraying bastard who had made her fall for him and then left her like she meant nothing. She was so over him and didn't want to see him again.

She kept walking, determined to start her new life away from them. The local library had already hired her, and she was due to start work Monday. Her independence was around the corner.

"Are you fucking deaf?" Murphy asked, grabbing her arm and halting her progress.

Snatching her arm out of his grip she turned to walk away.

"You're walking away like a fucking child. You may be grown up, Tate, but you're just a spoilt fucking, baby."

Tate stopped, turned and stormed back toward him. "I may be a baby, but at least my vocabulary is better than yours, you stupid bastard." Angered at his presence she lashed out and shoved him.

Murphy didn't go anywhere. He stayed put.

"We need to talk," he said.

Shaking her head, she headed in the other direction.

"You can't keep running from me, Tate. You need to hear my side."

She stopped and stared along the street, which was visible by the street lights.

"Go on then, let me hear your side." Folding her arms under her breasts she stood and waited for him to explain. This man had hurt her deeply by his deception.

"The club needed my help. They needed a man who could infiltrate the Lions."

Throwing her arms up in the air, Tate had heard enough. "It's always about the club, isn't it?"

"I came back for you. I did this to keep you safe," he said, stepping closer.

"No, you did this for the club."

"I care about you, Tate."

"No, if you cared about me you'd have found some way to tell me. You got up and just left, Murphy. You promised me you'd be there for me no matter what. We were supposed to be together, and you just left. You don't care about me. The only person you care about is yourself."

She turned to walk away and found herself pressed up against the wall. Murphy invaded her space, standing too close for her comfort. "I did what I had to in order to save the club. I care about you, and not a moment went by when I wasn't thinking about you."

Tears sprang to her eyes.

"Then look me in the eye and tell me you didn't fuck any of the women?" she asked.

He jolted as if she'd hit him. Murphy couldn't look at her.

"Tate, that's in the past."

She slapped him hard around the face, and he let her. "No, we're in the past."

"We can get past this."

"No."

"I was putting the club first," he said.

"And that's your problem. You will always put the club first. I've lived my whole life with a man who has put the club first. The Skulls always come first like it's some kind of sacred group." She stared into his eyes, knowing this was long overdue. "I've watched him hurt a woman he loves because of it. I'm not going to be second best, Murphy. I'm going to find a man where I come first."

His arms released her, and he let her go. She brushed past him, but he caught her hand and tugged her close. Tate collided with his body. Before she could breathe, his lips were on hers.

She gasped when he broke the kiss. "You may try to be with another man, Tate. You may even fall in love with him, but you and I both know, I'll always be your man just like you're my woman."

He let her go. The instant his arms left her she felt alone.

Murphy's words were true. She'd given her heart to him a long time ago. He knew stuff about her no one else would ever know. Rubbing her arms, she turned away and started walking.

She was walking toward a future and—she hoped—her future happiness.

The End

www.samcrescent.wordpress.com

Evernight Publishing

www.evernightpublishing.com

14827334R00100

Printed in Great Britain
by Amazon.co.uk, Ltd.,
Marston Gate.